The Styx Trilogy
Book One

Miscast Spells

by
Rose Corcoran

Printed in the United States of America

First Printing, 2015

ISBN 978-1-943798-06-3

www.rosecorcoranwrites.com

To
Mom, Dad,
Claire, Thomas,
and John Paul

♠♦♣♥♣♦♠

Table of Contents

Prologue

One Year and Two Months Ago

The golden afternoon sunlight streamed through the trees and onto the table, and the tea inspector's steady voice rose and fell as he told his tale. Everything was as peaceful and pleasant as could be—for Emmaline, at least. She could not say the same for Bostwick, whom she had last seen sulking around the halls of the palace, looking despondently into his empty top hat. She'd been tempted to invite him to lunch with them, but thought that Mr. Charles's lessons about some of the more obscure aspects of the tea trade might not be the best way to cheer someone up.

"…and that's where Dragon Well tea gets its name," Mr. Charles was saying. "But I wonder if you've ever heard of the Drink of the Immortals?"

"Is that supposed to be some kind of elixir of life?" Emmaline asked.

"It's actually just a particularly earthy variety of pu-erh. Never touch the stuff myself. Anyway, the interesting part is not the tea, but the creature it's named for: immortal beasts."

"What are they?"

"Mmm, it's hard to say," he said unctuously. He often used this tone of voice when negotiating with a client. "Are they goblins, or something else? No one knows. Long ago, humans and goblins alike told stories of strange beings, shape-shifters who never died and who, in no one's memory, were ever born. Some said they were doppelgangers who imitated mortal beings and took their places, influencing the powers and politics of countries across the globe."

"Why would they do that?" Emmaline asked, wide eyed.

Mr. Charles shrugged. "I guess if you live forever, you need a hobby. Anyway, humans stopped believing in such things long ago, but goblins still tell the tale of these mysterious people who may still walk the earth."

He took another sip of tea, then began to spread cream on one of the scones.

"So…?" Emmaline asked, wondering where he was going with all this. She enjoyed Mr. Charles's stories, but there were times when his point was opaque.

"That's all, really. I'm no expert on such things. I just thought it was an interesting story. But I'm sure a thirteen-year-old doesn't want to hear about some long dead creatures."

"If they're immortal, how can they be long dead?"

"Just checking to see if you were paying attention. You were, of course, but something else is on your mind. You were staring very seriously into your teacup a moment ago."

"I was just thinking about Bostwick."

"Ah, yes, the new court magician."

"He seems so gloomy all the time, and he's always thinking about that one spell."

"Well, some people like brooding over things they'll never be able to do," the tea inspector said, pouring his fourth cup of tea.

"It doesn't seem like he *likes* doing it at all. I just wish there was some way we could take his mind off it, but I'm not really sure what he's interested in. I haven't been able to talk to him very much, so—"

"It looks like this might be your chance," Mr. Charles said, waving at someone behind her. She turned to see a brown-haired boy in a tailcoat coming towards them. He looked vaguely annoyed at life in general, far too world-weary for his sixteen years.

"Hello, von Dogsbody," Mr. Charles said, though Emmaline knew Bostwick hated being referred to by his last name. "You seem peachy today. What's up?"

"You're late for some meeting about Earl Grey."

Mr. Charles looked confused for a moment, as if he was desperately trying to remember who Earl Grey was. Then he snapped his fingers, rose, and clapped Bostwick on his shoulder.

"That's right. I forgot all about it. Thanks for the tip, Dogsbody."

"Why can't you just call me Bostwick?" he asked in exasperation.

"'Dogsbody' is so much easier to remember. Anyway, since you're already out here, why don't you stay and tell the princess about the history of magic? You'll find she's quite bright," he added when Bostwick cast a skeptical glance her way. "Besides, it's your job to entertain the royal family."

"With spells, not history," Bostwick mumbled, taking Mr. Charles's seat as the tea inspector whisked away through the garden.

"I like history," Emmaline said, pushing the plate of scones over to him. He took one and began munching on it. This seemed to mollify him, so she continued. "I already know about how the invasion of goblins from Ataxia is what forced the human nations to join forces. It actually benefited humanity in the long run, because now everyone in the Empire has access to things like chocolate and lemons. We never would have been able to get those in Camellia originally, and we can trade our tea to other countries without worrying about bandits or tariffs or—"

She stopped, noticing that Bostwick's look of irritation had returned. As she suspected, Mr. Charles's brand of history—one that focused on trade—was a very acquired taste, and not one the magician seemed to enjoy.

"Um, anyway, Mr. Charles said that even when they formed the Empire, humans were still no match for goblins, so that's why Melieh had to find a way for humans to do magic."

"Sounds like you already know a lot about this," Bostwick said, with the air of a mechanic who had been called out to fix a perfectly functioning machine.

"But what I don't understand is how Melieh learned to do spells in the first place."

"Technically, he always could. Magicians are born with the potential to perform magic, but without training, it's too unpredictable and dangerous. That's probably why goblins like it so much—though I hear they can control their magic without even trying... Anyway, Melieh was just the first human who learned how to do specific spells and tricks."

"But *how?*"

"I don't know... practice? Look, goblins liked casting spells on humans, humans learned to cast their own spells, and goblins were so offended by that fact that they left the Empire for good. That's pretty much all you need to know about magic, as far as history is concerned."

Emmaline was not entirely satisfied with this paltry explanation, most of which she knew already, but was glad that Bostwick seemed to be in slightly better spirits... at least until he tried to pour himself a cup of tea; Mr. Charles had emptied the pot earlier.

"Um, we can re-steep it," Emmaline said, pulling the teapot over to the samovar. "While we wait, do you want to see the tea fields?"

"No, thanks." He stared at his empty cup like it had rendered him a personal insult, and Emmaline decided that she had had enough of his gloominess for one afternoon.

"You know, Bostwick, things could be worse," she said, standing and brushing some scone crumbs off her dress. "You could have to deal with an army of marauding goblins."

"...uh-huh."

"Or an immortal beast."

"Huh?"

"Never mind."

She strolled away from the tea table and followed a stone path past red and orange rose bushes until it sloped down to a low stone wall that looked out over the Principality of Camellia. The hills across from her were green with row upon row of well kept tea bushes. Emmaline breathed in, smelling flowers blended with the scent of fresh-cut foliage.

I wish Bostwick would focus on this sort of thing, she thought, *but I guess I can at least have one cup of tea with him, even if he won't cheer up.*

She spun around to return to the table, and felt something strange underfoot. Looking down, she saw that she was standing on what resembled a rat tail, though it was at least three feet long and continued into the bushes. She stepped off and followed it through the garden where it twisted around trees and flowerbeds until it finally connected to the backside of a short, furry creature with huge ears. At first Emmaline thought it was some sort of possum, until it turned to her and revealed a squashed, flat face with a malevolent expression. Though she had never seen one before, she knew immediately that it must be a goblin.

"Oh, um, is this your tail?" she said.

"Yeah," said the goblin. "And you just stepped on it."

Before Emmaline could apologize, the goblin snapped his stubby fingers, grinned at her, and ran toward the edge of the garden with his tail trailing behind him. Not wanting to lose sight of the first goblin she had ever seen, Emmaline started after him but tripped on the hem of her skirt—despite the fact that a moment ago it had been just below her knees. It felt like her entire dress was trying to swallow her, and soon her collar covered her face so that she couldn't see a thing. What was more, the fabric had become so heavy that she had difficulty fighting her way out.

"Bostwick!" she called, hoping that he hadn't left the garden.

My first encounter with a goblin, she thought, finally managing to get her head out of one of the sleeves, *and he turns my dress enormous. No wonder the Empire expelled them.*

"Emmaline?" Bostwick said, coming down the path. "Did you ca—ahh!"

He cringed away from her as she looked up at him—very far up. He towered over her, then knelt down, appearing huge.

"Oh no!" she said. "Bostwick, don't tell me that thing shrank me. It shrank me, didn't it?"

"Um, not exactly," he said.

"What happened then? Why is everything so, so…"

Bostwick scooped her up, clothes and all, and said, "I think we should talk to your parents."

One

The Butler Did It

No trespassers, scallywags, librarians, or shoemakers! To enter castle, please ring bell. To ring bell, please knock! the sign on the enormous wooden door said. Bostwick rapped on the wood and heard a giant bell ringing deep within the recesses of the castle.

"'Knock to ring the bell'," he said. "What is wrong with goblins? Everyone on this whole continent is insane."

"Well, if this works, we'll be able to go home soon," Emmaline said.

"*If* it works, which I highly doubt. We've been traveling through Ataxia for a year without so much as a clue to breaking your curse, and suddenly we're supposed to believe that what we needed all along is in the country right across the Empire's border? I'm not even sure this so called Domino of Nonpareil even exists, despite what—"

He was cut off by the creaking of the door. He hastily shoved Emmaline under his top hat and fell silent. The person opening the door was a girl around Emmaline's age who looked liked an ordinary human except for her short green hair. Over a gray dress she wore a white apron, and under green eyes, she wore a smile.

"Hello," she said in a soft, sweet voice. "Welcome to Castle Styx, Home of Queen Delilah Glossolalia. What can I do for you?"

"My name is Bostwick von Dogsbody, and I am a door-to-door magician."

"Door-to-door magician?" she asked with a bewildered expression. "What do you want—er, well, what are you doing here?"

"I'm selling magic tricks. Door-to-door," Bostwick said, and added quietly to himself, "obviously."

"Like a real magic show!" she said excitedly, then took a breath to calm herself down. "I'm sure Delilah would love that. Come in, won't you?"

Bostwick and the be-hatted Emmaline entered the castle. The walls were covered by what looked like huge playing cards, and the floor was tiled in dominoes. *They have a bit of a game obsession*, thought Bostwick, who had noticed the chess piece topiary on the castle grounds. As peculiar as this was, it was far from the strangest motif he had ever encountered in a goblin dwelling. He also noticed that unlike most of the musty buildings he had found himself in over the past year, this castle had a pleasant, slightly fruity scent and was devoid of the usual clutter and chaos associated with goblins.

"So, who exactly are you?" Bostwick asked, wondering how much this presumably human girl had contributed to the civilized state of the castle.

"Oh," said the girl, looking slightly embarrassed, "my name's Millicent. I'm the maid."

"And the doorman, also, apparently."

"Oh, yes, and the gardener, and the cook, and a number of other things, but 'maid' is a lot easier to say than all that, so there you are."

"I see," said Bostwick, though he didn't. "So this queen, what's she like?"

"Oh, she's very nice, and, well, some might call her eccentric—"

Which translates to crazy, thought Bostwick.

"—but she's actually really level-headed, I think."

"You think?"

"Oh, I meant—"

"Stop saying 'oh' all the time. And if you think something's true, say so without saying it's what you think, because we gathered that already."

Millicent looked surprised, then defeated.

"Oh," she said.

Although Emmaline couldn't see a thing, she certainly heard the sadness in the girl's voice, and gave Bostwick a sharp kick to the top of the head. He yelled out in pain and his hat dropped to the floor, which caused Emmaline to come rolling out of it.

"A white rabbit!" cried Millicent. "Hello!"

The rabbit said nothing, but glared angrily at Bostwick.

"That's mine," he said. "Standard issue for magicians like me."

"Wow! What's its name?"

"Emmaline."

"She's so cute! Can I hold her?"

"Ah, she may look cute, but she's actually *very* ill tempered," he said, returning the rabbit's nasty look. "She'd probably try to take your arm off if you tried to touch her."

"Oh," Millicent began, but immediately stopped and looked apologetic. "I mean… 'Aha', but I'm very good with animals. I've never met one who didn't like me."

"That may be so, but this rabbit doesn't like to be carried around by just anybody."

No sooner had he said this, however, than the rabbit hopped into Millicent's arms and, unseen by the maid, stuck her tongue out at Bostwick.

"Fine," he said, "if you want to be that way about it."

"I'm sorry. I'll put her down if…"

"I wasn't talking to you, I was talking to her." He gestured at the rabbit, who was innocently sniffing in Millicent's apron pocket.

"Oh," she said thoughtfully, then realized what she'd just said. "I mean, no, um, oh… oh, I'm sorry, I'm just so used to saying it!"

"What?" asked Bostwick, perplexed.

"I keep saying 'oh', but you said it annoys you, so I tried to stop saying it, but I'm no good at not saying it, you see?"

The insanity is spreading, Bostwick thought, as he watched the girl become more and more flustered, and Emmaline shot him dirty looks that said, *Bostwick, you're inhuman, even more so than me*—looks which penetrated into his very core and, well, made him feel a little guilty.

"Wait, wait, stop. I didn't mean don't say 'oh' ever again, I just meant… Look, I shouldn't have said anything. Sorry."

"How terribly touching," said an oily voice from out of nowhere. Suddenly, one of the hearts from the playing card wallpaper floated off the wall and up to Bostwick, then in a swoosh of color, turned into a woman. The first thing he noticed was that she wore a plain black masquerade mask. It looked so simple, and yet he knew it must have been what he and Emmaline had been searching for. But even though this mask was the answer to all their problems, Bostwick couldn't focus on it for long before noticing the eyes framed behind it that were staring back at him—large, yellow, snake-pupil eyes.

Bostwick finally stepped back to look at the woman entirely. She stood slightly taller than him, though she leaned back on one hip, making her appear several inches shorter. The purples and pinks of her form-fitting dress splashed and swirled around each other with no discernible rhyme or reason, and her bubblegum pink hair spiked up and fell down, creating a giant cascade of color on her head, almost hiding her two long, pointed ears.

Bostwick and Emmaline exchanged knowing looks, but said nothing.

"So, Millicent," the masked woman, whom Bostwick assumed was the queen, said, "who is this foul-natured young man so prone to hasty apologies, hmm?"

"He's Bostwick, a door-to-door magician."

"Really? Bostwick, eh? Sounds more like a name for a butler. You know," she said, leaning her wild face right into his, "I'm in need of a butler."

"I only do magic," he said, starting to get annoyed again.

"In that case, you may be my court magician. That's a more respectable position than door-to-door."

This made Bostwick clench his teeth.

"I think my profession is quite respectable, thank you."

"Fine, be that way. Whatever kind of magician you are,

let's see some of your tricks."

"All right, let's begin."

"What? Here?" the queen asked incredulously, as if he'd suggested doing teppanyaki at a funeral.

"What's wrong with here?"

"Silly, silly magician," she said in a sing-song voice. "Are we to be entertained in the hallway like the common rabble who are unfortunate enough not to own palaces? Certainly not! We shall retire to the throne room and carry on the festivities there."

Not caring to argue, Bostwick followed the queen and Millicent to the throne room. This was in no way a linear journey, however. The group wandered around the castle at the queen's will, going from the card hallway to a giant library full of nothing but cookbooks. Bostwick caught a glimpse of *All Slime and No Spine: Creating Proper Cactus Cuisine* and *101 Semi-Edible Mushrooms* before being shoved toward a ladder that led down a hole in the floor. They found themselves in a network of caves lit with gaslights around the walls, and Delilah launched into a rambling story about some incident involving bugbears and a bomb scare in the town.

"...and if you're going to *plant* a bomb, you had better make sure it blows up, otherwise it's a nuisance for everyone involved," she concluded. Bostwick was grateful that he hadn't really been listening. He wondered briefly if this mad woman really was the queen, or just some impersonator let loose in the castle. Either way, that mask on her face looked a lot like the one Emmaline needed, and it didn't matter who it belonged to at the moment, so long as he got it in the end.

They finally went up a winding staircase, and Bostwick let

out an exasperated sigh when he saw that they were back in the card hallway where they had started.

"Ah, here we are," Delilah said, sliding the eight of clubs aside to reveal a small doorway. "I knew we'd find it eventually."

"You mean all that time, you were looking for your own throne room?" asked Bostwick.

"Don't be absurd. Our throne room doesn't move around. That would be bothersome."

"But why—"

"Before you go asking silly questions," replied the queen, "I shall respond with an equally silly answer. What one is searching for is always in the last place one looks."

"But it could have been the first place we looked!"

"That," she said with finality, "is ridiculous. Now, through the door you go."

Grumbling to himself, Bostwick ducked through the door, followed by the rest. They found a small shaft with a ladder leading up to a trapdoor that opened up into a room as tall and wide as the inside of a chapel. The floor was shining black and white checkered marble and the ceiling was vaulted. One wall of the room, to their left, was taken up almost entirely by a grand double door, which Bostwick wished they had used instead of this ridiculous entrance. The wall behind them and the one across from it were covered in a mosaic of mirrors, marbles and stone set in no particular pattern, all green and yellow. The most spectacular wall of all, however, was the fourth, which was not so much a wall as a gigantic, stained-glass clock with working hands and gears. Directly in front of this was a set of smooth stone steps, upon which sat the throne. The seat and arms were cushioned as a standard armchair would be, but the back rose magnificently in the shape of a Gothic arch, topped by a menacing series of green spikes. On closer inspection, Bostwick saw that the throne was neither grand nor sinister, but instead looked like nothing more or less than a common pineapple.

"Well, let's have that magic show," said Delilah, who flounced over to the throne and sat down. She placed her hands on each arm of the chair, grandly surveying the room, then skooched entirely to one side and patted the portion of seat next to her. "Come here, Millie. We'll watch together."

"Here's your rabbit back," said Millicent, carefully holding her at arm's length for Bostwick to take. "Good luck!"

She went to join Delilah, while Bostwick set Emmaline on his shoulder and straightened his tail coat and bow tie.

"Listen, I think we should just take the mask and go," he whispered to Emmaline.

"We'll do no such thing. Just ask for it without rousing suspicion." She hopped to the ground, her paws skittering on the smooth floor. "We'll decide what to do from there."

"Right," he said, unsure of how to "just ask for it". He checked to see how closely the queen and her maid where watching him. Delilah was focused on smoothing out her dress, but Millicent was leaning forward on the throne, clutching her skirt in anticipation. The fact that at least one person was excited to see his magic show gave him a boost of confidence.

He took a breath, put his hat on his head, and held his hand out to the side.

"Ladies and…well, ladies, allow me to begin. Magic, as you may know, is both an art, and a science, delicate in both—"

"Hold it!" cried Delilah.

"What?"

"How does this work? Am I paying you by the hour, or what?"

"Yes, by the hour."

"Then cut the chit chat and move on to the tricks."

"Very well, *Your Majesty*. This first trick involves…"

"That wasn't very nice, Delilah," Millicent said quietly while Bostwick elaborated what he was going to do.

"You know, my dear, he's not very nice either, so I figure I can relax the rules of politeness a little."

"I'm sure he's not as bad as he seems."

"You give him too much credit, I think."

"Well… We hardly know him. Maybe he's just having a bad day?"

"You always think the best of people, don't you, Millie? It's a lovely quality to have, but I wonder if it's for your own good."

"Are you two even listening?" Bostwick said.

"You were saying stuff about this'n'that, or something, right?" said Delilah.

"Just watch." Bostwick spun on his heel and walked into the center of the room. With a wave of his hand, the lights went out, leaving him bathed in the green and yellow glow from the stained glass clock. Delilah and Millicent oohed and clapped.

"That wasn't the trick, yet. I'm just setting the mood,"

growled Bostwick. "Now, watch and be amazed."

From a pocket in his tailcoat, he pulled a plain handkerchief and placed it over his hand. He then removed it with a flourish to reveal a shiny pocket watch.

"Why," said the queen, "that's my watch that I lost this morning! What a marvelous trick!"

"It is not yours! And the trick still isn't over. Now observe."

He threw the watch to the ground, breaking the lid off its hinge. As if that wasn't enough, Bostwick then produced a large mallet, seemingly out of nowhere, and proceeded to hammer the watch into pieces.

"Now this I like," said Delilah.

Once the watch was demolished, Bostwick swept its remains into a dustpan he had conjured and poured them into his hat. He waved his hand over the hat and, finally, pulled out the watch, perfectly intact and ticking.

"That's amazing!" Millicent said. "I wish I could do that to all the stuff I break."

"Yes, yes, this pleases me," said Delilah. "Do continue, magician."

And continue he did. He performed tricks using handkerchief ropes and spells involving the conjuration and vanishment of birds. He made bouquets of flowers appear and turned bowling pins into vases to hold them. He had just finished a card trick involving the ace of hearts when he decided to make his move.

"For my final trick, I'll need an item from a volunteer."

"I don't think I have anything worth using magic on," said Millicent, who began to frantically search her apron pockets. "I have some cards, but you already did a trick like that."

"How about your mask, Your Majesty?" Bostwick asked in the most innocent tone he could muster.

"It's called a domino, this mask is," she said proudly.

"All right, your domino, then." He was now almost certain it was the one he needed.

"No can do. It's a family heirloom, and after what you did to that watch, I wouldn't trust you with my bedroom slippers."

"But the watch turned out all right."

"Ah, but what if it hadn't? A watch is easy to replace, but not so my domino."

"What's so special about it?" he dared to ask, afraid his eagerness would show.

"Hmm," she said with a shrug, "who can say?"

This mysterious response only confirmed his suspicions; now he just had to figure out a way to get the mask without being caught.

"Very well, I'll use something else."

"I have a better idea. Since this is your last trick, I want to see something fun. Something I've always wanted to see, but in all my many years was never given the chance."

"Um..." said Bostwick, getting an unpleasant feeling.

"Oh, don't worry. It'll be easy for one as accomplished as you."

Oh no, thought Bostwick, *not this time.*

"I want you to pull a rabbit out of your hat."

Here we go, Bostwick thought, reaching for his hat, which Emmaline had crawled back into when no one was looking.

He held out the hat in front of him and waved his hand vaguely over it. Without a word, he reached in and pulled out the rabbit, who hopped to the ground. Millicent's applause was cut short by the queen.

"Hold it!" Delilah said. "That's the same rabbit from before!"

"Well, yeah. She's my rabbit," Bostwick said. "I always use her in this trick."

"Well, I want another rabbit! Like a brown one, maybe."

"Look, I'm not doing the trick again. It's really… complicated."

"What's so complicated about pulling a rabbit out of a hat? If I'm paying for this show, I wanna brown, never-before-seen rabbit."

"Well, I'll need some time to prepare."

"You didn't have to prepare before, you just…" but she trailed off, looking like she'd just realized something incredible.

The room suddenly became colder and darker, or at least that's how it seemed to Bostwick. He knew he'd been discovered but dreaded what would happen next. The queen's expression changed from shock to a combination of smugness, anger, amusement, and accusation. It was terrifying.

"You can't pull a rabbit from a hat, at least not magically, can you?" she said in a voice as cold as ice. She stood up from her throne and walked over to Bostwick. Looking down her nose at him, she asked, "What kind of magician are you, anyway?"

At this, Bostwick became impudent.

"I'm an excellent magician! I just can't do that stupid parlor trick."

"And here I thought you made your living out of stupid parlor tricks."

Having no response to this, Bostwick grabbed his props, shoved his hat on, and turned to leave.

"And where do you think you're going?" asked the queen in a hideously smug voice.

"Since you won't be paying me, and you obviously don't want to see any more tricks…"

"Who said I won't be paying you? I shall give you what is due. After all," she said with a grin from ear to ear, "you're an *excellent* magician."

"Forget it. I don't need your money," said Bostwick, whose pride mattered more than his pocketbook.

He continued out through the gigantic double door and into a hallway full of portraits of pointy-eared, snake-eyed people doing ridiculous and dangerous things. Without thinking where he was going, he walked to the end of the hall, which opened into a small greenhouse. Looking around at the various species of plants, Bostwick realized he hadn't a clue how to get out of the castle. He decided to try and go back the way he came, spun around, and crashed into Millicent, knocking them both to the ground.

"Ah, sorry! What—?" Bostwick began.

"You forgot your rabbit," she said, holding Emmaline out to him.

"Oh my gosh! I'm so sorry, Emmaline!"

She responded by hopping to him and chomping his finger. Bostwick did not respond, so Emmaline looked up at him apologetically and nudged his hand with her nose.

"She's trying to make you feel better," said Millicent. "What a nice rabbit."

"Don't bother," he said to Emmaline.

"I'm sorry Delilah was so cruel back there. I guess it's her goblin nature."

"You'd think the human in her would make her a little more civilized, though."

"She doesn't have any human in her. She's full-blooded goblin royalty."

"Oh. I just assumed with the way other goblins talk about Styx… They say it's a backwater, that the royalty aren't fit to be goblins, consorting with humans and other mongrels." Emmaline bit his hand again. "Ow! Well, anyway, she doesn't look much like the goblins anywhere else in Ataxia. Other than her eyes and ears, she looks human."

"You shouldn't say that to her. She'd be very insulted."

"Hmm," he said, considering if that was really a bad thing.

"Don't let what she said bother you. You really did do some amazing magic."

"But she's right. What kind of magician can't pull a rabbit out of a hat? The very idea is absurd. I don't even understand it myself."

"Maybe if you practice?"

"I've tried that. I don't know what it is, but I've never been able to do it."

"But you can do all the other tricks, right?"

"Yeah."

"So why worry?"

Why worry indeed? he thought. That's what Emmaline had said, too. How could he explain it to them? Sure, the trick was rather dull and useless, but it was also at the heart of what it meant to be a magician. Not being able to do that trick was like not being able to say the word "is." Either way, one would be lacking something basic to his vocabulary. Unfortunately, non-magicians didn't grasp this concept.

"Yes, I suppose I shouldn't worry," Bostwick forced himself to say. "Well, thank you for bringing me my rabbit. I should probably be leaving."

"Wait, I'm also supposed to give you this." She held out a sack full of coins. "For the magic show. And Delilah said if you don't accept it, I should 'chuck it at your head', so you really should take it."

"How delightful," he said, standing up and holding out his hand. "Here."

Millicent gave him the bag.

"Actually, I was offering to help you up, but…"

"Oh!" said Millicent, who turned pink and grabbed his hand, then proceeded to turn scarlet. "Thank you."

"Sure," he said nonchalantly, helping her up.

"Um, Delilah also said that to make up for her, um, 'completely justified and enjoyable rudeness', to offer to let you stay the night in her castle."

"Or she'll chuck it at my head?"

"Something like that."

"I guess I have no choice."

He followed Millicent back into the hall of portraits. They stopped in front of a painting of a rotund goblin kissing a toad delicately on the head, which the maid pulled aside to reveal a hidden staircase. They took this up to the next floor, where they entered yet another hallway with a number of doors on either side, as well as a few on the ceiling.

"Your room is the third on the right. If you need anything, just ring the bell." With that, Millicent left through the door through which they'd come.

Bostwick and the rabbit entered the room, which, it turned out, was the most normal in the castle. It had one window overlooking the garden. and contained nothing more than a bed, a table and chairs, and a vase of flowers.

"Well," said Bostwick, locking the door behind him, "I think this is a golden opportunity."

"You'd better not be thinking of stealing that mask," Emmaline said.

"And how do you propose we get it? That mad queen didn't seem too likely to want to give it up."

"Maybe we can use it once to get me back to normal."

"That won't work, Emmaline. The legend says the Domino of Nonpareil only gives power to whoever wears it. You'd have to have it on for the rest of your life."

"We can at least try."

"But what if it doesn't work? Are you just going to give up?"

"We'll find something else." Bostwick rolled his eyes. "Still, I should try it on. We'll go tonight when everyone's asleep."

"One problem," said Bostwick. "We have no idea where she keeps it at night."

♣♦♣♥♣♦♣

Getting a map of the castle turned out to be fairly easy. Bostwick rang the bell to summon Millicent, who brought him one without question. As soon as she left, he and Emmaline got to work.

"Let's see... If she keeps it with her, it would probably be in her bedroom," said Bostwick. "That's up in the main tower."

"What if she takes it off at night?"

"In that case, it'd be in the treasure chamber which is... below the ballroom? I can't tell if this line is a walkway or a wall or what. Who in the world drew this?"

"It does look kind of scribbly," said Emmaline, who was trying to decide if the thing at the bottom of the map was part of the castle, the compass, or just some spilled coffee. "I think if we take this secret passage from our hallway, it should bring us to a staircase that leads straight up to her bedroom. We should start there, since we know where it is. And if she's still awake, we can duck onto this walkway that leads to the ballroom without being seen."

They waited until midnight, then made their way silently to the tower. On the way, they saw no guards or people of any kind. Apparently, only the queen and Millicent lived here which, although strange, made the job of sneaking around at night that much easier. They reached the doorway leading to the tower and started up the spiral staircase, passing doors with all sorts of labels, such as *Ballroom, Laboratory,* and *The Loo.* When they reached the top-most door, it read *Delilah's Room. No boys allowed. Keep out!*

Bostwick quietly opened the door, which was not locked. The room within was vast and dark, and they could only make out vague shapes of what must have been furniture. Bostwick snapped his fingers and a small flame appeared in his hand. By the dim light they could see that the room was furnished with a vanity, several decorative vases, and a small table with two armchairs in front of a good-sized fireplace. There was also a tall window with curtains blocking out whatever moonlight there was that night. And, finally, there was a large, four poster bed, on which lay the queen, who was fast asleep. She was still wearing the Domino.

Bostwick carefully approached her. With her reptilian eyes closed she looked almost human, but not enough to make Bostwick let down his guard. He stopped when he was still several feet from the bed and extinguished the flame to avoid waking her. Then, ever so carefully, he reached forward and, barely touching her face, removed the mask.

Without a word, he crept back to the door where Emmaline sat. The Domino was much too big for her rabbit face, but he held it in place for her. They both held their breath.

"H-how do I make it work?" Emmaline whispered.

"Try picturing how you used to look and will yourself to become that. That's what I'd do."

It took a few seconds. Suddenly, the Domino seemed to melt away and disappear, while Emmaline transformed in a swoosh, just as Delilah had when she first appeared as a playing card heart. Where a rabbit had once been now sat a teenage girl. Her curly blonde hair fell to her waist and her silver dress had white rabbit fur around the collar and sleeves.

"You still have rabbit ears," said Bostwick.

"Well, I've gotten used to them, you know? They're great

for hearing, and so cute." Bostwick grimaced. "Fine, have it your way," she said. She shut her eyes, concentrating, and the ears vanished.

"Good. Now, take it off and see if you change back."

"Um." She reached up to her now human face. "I can't."

"What do you mean?"

"I don't know. I know I'm wearing the mask, but I can't feel it on my face. It's like it's disappeared."

"I can't see it either. Maybe it's only visible if you're not using it to turn into anything. I guess that makes sense. You wouldn't want a mask to show up on everything you changed into, would you? That's clever."

"It's awful. This means I have to keep the mask to stay this way."

"Honestly, Emmaline, you're a lot more deserving of it than that queen."

"But it's not mine, no matter how much I deserve it."

"We're taking it."

"No, we are not. I'm the one who needs it, so it's my decision."

"I'm the one who has to work as a lowly door-to-door magician while you're in rabbit form, so it's *my* decision. Plus, I'm bigger than you no matter what shape you are," he said, and picked her up in his arms. "Let's go."

"How dare you! I command you to put me down this instant!"

"No," he said, but as soon as he took his first wobbly step towards the door it became obvious that no matter how big he was, he definitely wasn't strong enough to carry the struggling, human-sized Emmaline. On his second step, he fell right over backwards and crashed into one of the vases. At the sound of the crash, Delilah leapt up and turned her bedside gas lamp up to illuminate the intruders, while Bostwick and Emmaline froze in terror. They stared at each other for what seemed an eternity.

"Who are you?" Delilah finally asked.

"We're just, um," Bostwick began, but was cut off.

"Wait a minute. You're that lousy magician who can't do the hat trick, right?"

"Yes, indeed, and I was just—"

"Then who are *you*?" she nodded toward Emmaline.

"She's my assistant," Bostwick said, "and we were just… lost. You see, we have a pressing engagement and really can't stay."

"But… this is my bedroom," she said, yawning.

"Like I said, we got lost."

"But… we're at the top of the tower."

"Well, uh," said Bostwick, struggling for a halfway decent explanation, "we came to ask you for directions."

"If you were lost, how'd you find my room? And why'd you break my vase?" she asked, and rubbed her eyes, which widened in shock, "and where's my Domino!"

She grabbed Bostwick by the collar and wrenched him up from the floor.

"You thieving little worm. You stole my Domino right off my face!"

"No, I—"

"Do you know what happens to thieves around these parts, hmm?"

"They go to prison?" asked Bostwick hopefully.

"Ah, yes, the lucky ones go to prison, also known as the castle dungeon, but not your kind. Stealing a magical artifact from a goblin queen is no mere act of theft. It is a sacrilege, and for such a crime my ancestors would have cursed you where you stood."

"Wait!" cried Emmaline. "You can't!"

"Oh?"

"Please, it's my fault. I asked him to get me the Domino. Without it..."

She transformed back into a rabbit, and the mask reappeared and fell to the ground. Delilah released Bostwick from her grasp.

"Who are you *really*?"

"My name is Princess Emmaline Camellia, twelfth heir of the Principality of Camellia. I was cursed by a goblin and turned into a rabbit. My true form is as the girl you saw before. We've been searching for a way to turn me back, and heard about the Domino of Nonpareil. Please don't punish Bostwick. He's my family's court magician, so he has to do what I say, and I told him to get it for me. So you see, I'm the one who took it."

"You took it? I find that hard to believe. You're obviously an honest person, while this one," she said, gesturing to Bostwick, "is clearly a scoundrel and a scallywag."

"Oh, but he's not, I assure you!"

"Silence! We'll see if you're telling the truth. Let's ask an impartial observer."

She walked over to the vanity and placed her hand on the top frame of the mirror. Looking into it, she said, "Show me."

The image in the mirror, which had previously reflected the queen, with the bed and door to the room in the background, rippled and changed. It reflected the same spot in the room, only now the queen was asleep in bed with her back to the mirror. Emmaline and Bostwick watched in amazement as the reflection showed them come through the door just as they'd done a few minutes ago.

"This mirror shows what happened in the past?" Bostwick asked.

"It's good to reflect back on one's memories every so often," said Delilah stoically, then added, "It's also handy for catching burglars. Like right here."

The mirror had just shown Bostwick removing the mask. They watched as Emmaline transformed, she and Bostwick had a silent argument, and he picked her up.

"Strange," said Delilah to Emmaline. "It looked a bit like you didn't want to take my Domino. Or maybe you ordered him to carry you out of the room, hmm? The jig is up."

"Very well," said Bostwick. "I won't argue with your mirror. What punishment did you have in store? You said something about a curse."

He looked extremely apprehensive and even cringed a little. Delilah looked him over, thinking for a moment, then smiled.

"No," she said. "Although it might be fun to curse you, I have a much more *interesting* idea. You shall serve under me in my castle, and do whatever I ask of you, for as long as the sentence lasts. If you try to escape or disobey, *then* you will be hit with whatever curse I deem appropriate."

"And that curse might be?"

"I think I'll just let you imagine that."

"And how long would I have to serve you?"

"Oh, let's say a hundred years; that's a nice round number. Agreed?" She held out her hand to shake on the deal.

Bostwick considered his options, but found that he didn't have any. If he was cursed, he would have no hope of finding a cure for Emmaline. Two rabbits wouldn't get far in Ataxia, and he suspected that the queen wouldn't shy away from an even nastier punishment than mere animal transformation. Though he wasn't fond of the idea, staying in this castle might lead to the discovery of a real way to break the curse, and in the absolute worst case scenario, he would still be close to the Domino if that was the only way.

Swallowing his pride, he shook the queen's hand.

"I agree."

"Glad to hear it. Oh," she said to Emmaline, "you can stay here, too, I guess."

Emmaline turned to Bostwick apologetically.

"I'm sorry, Bostwick. This is all my fault."

"No, you were right about not stealing it."

"Still, I hate to see you punished like this."

"Actually, it looks like I got off pretty easily. After all, it won't be so bad serving a hundred years as a court magician."

"A court magician? You?" scoffed Delilah. "Good chaos, no! You're just not court magician material."

"What? Then what exactly am I going to be doing?"

The queen smiled a sickening smile.

"You'll be my butler, of course. It suits you, *Bostwick*," she said with a chuckle. "This is going to be fun."

Two

A Confusing Crash Course in the History and Economics of Styx

The smell of bacon, eggs, and toast filled Millicent's senses as she carried the breakfast tray to Bostwick's room. She knocked on the door and was greeted by "Go away!"

"But, um, I have your breakfast," Millicent replied.

There was movement within the room and the door opened. Bostwick was already dressed. Instead of the tailcoat and burgundy cummerbund that he had worn the day before, he now wore a double-breasted vest and dress shirt.

"Sorry, I thought you were Emmaline," he said, gesturing for her to enter. "She's been coming by every five minutes trying to cheer me up."

Emmaline had been given the room next to Bostwick's. "It's just not proper for a lady rabbit to share a room with a gentleman, if you can call that guy a gentleman," was how Delilah had put it.

Millicent placed the tray on the table, next to the vase of roses, then went to the window and threw open the curtains, flooding the room with sunlight and cool air from the garden. Breathing it all in, she said, "It sure is a beautiful day."

"No day in Styx can be called beautiful," Bostwick said, sitting down at the table. "Thanks for breakfast, by the way."

"You're welcome."

Bostwick started to eat. Millicent fiddled with the tassel on the curtain ties as her eyes roved around the room. She wanted to start a conversation, but had no idea of what to talk about, so she decided to say the first thing that came to her mind.

"Are you really going to stay here for a hundred years?" Bostwick choked on his toast. "Sorry, I just... Delilah told me what happened last night. About the Domino, and you being our butler and, well, I sort of feel partially responsible."

"How is it your fault?" asked Bostwick, coughing.

Millicent flushed and looked away.

"Well, I was the one who gave you the map to the castle." It wasn't a complete lie, and there was no way she would tell him her own suspicions as to why Delilah had really made him stay in the castle.

"We would still have tried to find it, map or no map. You didn't do anything wrong. Delilah probably told you to bring us whatever we asked for, right?"

"Yeah," she said, relieved that he'd bought her story, and continued to turn the tassel over in her hands.

"Um, do you want any?" Bostwick asked, offering her the other piece of toast.

"No thank you. I already had breakfast with Delilah."

"Together?"

"We always have breakfast together."

"That sounds fun."

"Oh, it is!" Millicent said, not catching the sarcasm. "Delilah really isn't as bad as she tries to make herself out to be. Once you get to know her—"

But her praise was cut off by a yell from the hall.

"Booooooostwiiiiiiiiiick!"

Delilah burst through the door, carrying Emmaline on her head.

"*Bost*wick!" she cried flamboyantly. "Stop this dilly-dally! You've got lots of work to do."

With that, she grabbed his plate and flung it out the window, toast and all.

"Delilah," Millicent said calmly, "I was just telling Bostwick how you're *not* as crazy as you seem."

"Pshaw! What do I care for sanity, especially at a time like this? Do you know how filthy the upstairs library is? There are life forms in there that ought not be seen by human eyes, or smelt by human noses, or—"

"But you're not human," Bostwick said. "What do you care?"

"I don't. Actually, I enjoy it. But such an environment is not conducive to Millie's health. Clean it up, or you'll be out on the street faster than you can say 'poltroon'."

"Really?" Bostwick asked hopefully.

"No, not really. And if you bring it up again, I shall bestow such a curse on you, such a curse! I shall make it so the more you bathe, the filthier you become. Ha! How's that for mischief! That's high quality goblinical stuff!"

Bostwick thought it over.

"We'll clean your library, all right?" Emmaline chimed in, before Bostwick could decide.

"Why, I wouldn't dream of forcing a princess to do such menial labor. You shall sit and watch with me."

When they arrived at the upstairs library, which was located above the throne room, they saw that Delilah's description of it was no exaggeration. There were cobwebs hanging from shelf to shelf that were opaque with dirt. The floor was not visible due to books and debris scattered everywhere. Bostwick picked one book up and discovered a thick coating of dust on the cover. He attempted to open it, but the pages cracked and turned to powder before his eyes.

"Would you stop *destroying* my library," Delilah said from over his shoulder.

"I didn't mean to. I just… What are you doing?"

The queen was floating about three feet off the ground, leaning forward to look over his shoulder.

"I am hovering."

"How?"

"I'm a goblin, silly," she replied, and floated to the top of one of the bookshelves, where she delicately placed herself, sending showers of dust wafting to the ground.

"I've never seen any goblin fly without wings before."

"Ugh, flying without wings? How undignified. I float. I never fly, although, I confess, I would simply love to do so."

"But *how* do you float? Only the most skilled magicians can levitate people."

The queen merely smirked and said, "Peculiar. Now, get cleaning."

Bostwick surveyed the area and decided the fastest way to handle the situation would be to use magic. He took out a purple satin cloth from his top hat, threw it over one of the writing tables, drew a triangle in the air with his finger and pulled the cloth off, revealing the table and books left intact, but without a speck of dust to be seen.

"You vanished the dust!" Millicent exclaimed.

"But left everything else," said Delilah from her perch. "That's some exceptional magic."

Bostwick was about to say it was nothing really, but the queen added, "I can't imagine where a butler would learn something like that."

"You know, I was at the top of my class at Melieh's Academy of Magic."

"Mmm, and tell me, Bostwick, how did you come to be a student at such a prestigious school, considering your background?"

"What do you know about my background?"

"You are a commoner. I can tell these things."

Bostwick bristled, but continued on to the next filthy table. "For your information, I was accepted because the Academy recognized my talent."

"I see. And what were you before, hmm?"

"My parents own a stationery store in the Capital," he mumbled.

This made the queen laugh so hard she fell off the bookshelf and made a giant cloud of dust rise up from the floor.

"It's not funny."

"It's hilarious! You're telling me that humans actually

have stores for the specific purpose of selling paper? That's ridiculous!"

"Do you want to know how many absurd stores Emmaline and I have found traveling in Ataxia?"

"The most uncomfortable of which," said Emmaline, "was a shop devoted to the sale of hasenpfeffer."

"Anyway, it doesn't matter what my parents were," Bostwick continued, laying the cloth over the top of one of the bookshelves, "because *I* am a magician."

"It doesn't do to be ashamed of one's parentage," Delilah said.

"I'm not ashamed."

Bostwick left the conversation at that, because cleaning became a much more laborious chore. Finished with the tables, he moved on to one of the bookshelves, but after he removed the cloth, found a sticky film coating the surface of the wood, which refused to come off no matter what spell he tried.

"I've seen this before," Millicent said, prodding the goo with her finger. "It's mostly in the dungeon, though. Delilah, do you know what this is?"

"Nope."

"How am I supposed to clean it up?" asked Bostwick.

"No idea, but why don't I give Emmaline a tour of the castle while you figure it out, hmm? I'd stay and watch, but that would be boring."

She picked Emmaline up again and marched out of the room without another word.

"Finally," Bostwick said.

"Sorry," said Millicent. "She can be a bit abrasive. I've

learned over the years that that's just the way goblins are."

"Speaking of goblins, how is it that you came to work in Styx, or in Ataxia at all for that matter? I mean," he faltered, "you are human, right?"

"Yes! You could tell, even with my green hair?"

"Well, yeah. You're too nice-looking to be a goblin, and much too polite."

Millicent uttered an almost inaudible gasp and, had she the ability, would have started to glow. Bostwick noticed none of this, and continued.

"So why did you come to Styx?"

"Oh, right," she said hesitantly. "I came here because… Delilah wanted me here."

"Well, of course you wouldn't be here if Delilah didn't want you to be, but why did *you* want to work here?"

Millicent looked sheepish, and suddenly Bostwick realized that she was probably in the same boat he was. No sane person would ever, of his own free will, work for someone like Delilah. A sudden wave of pity washed over him. This poor, timid girl had probably committed some minor misdeed, like trampling on the queen's flowers or something, and was now pressed into who knew how many years of service. And now, he was rudely reminding her of her own misfortune.

"Uh, never mind," Bostwick said, pulling the cloth off another bookshelf. "We should probably be focusing on how to get that sticky stuff cleaned up."

"Right! Let me see."

Millicent went to one of the shelves and scanned its contents. She pulled out a mustard green book and opened it.

"What's that?" Bostwick asked.

"*Flora, Fauna, and Fungi of the Goblin World*. I'm fairly sure that goo came from some kind of animal."

It seemed to Bostwick that the maid must have lived among goblins for some time to assume something like that. He continued cleaning while Millicent read. Gradually, the room began to look more and more like a library and less like an abandoned catacomb. The polished cherry-wood shelves glinted softly in the light of the midday sun, and the bright blue carpet was visible between stacks of now dustless books. The only remaining things to be cleaned were some cobwebs high up in the corners of the ceiling and the mysteriously oily shelf.

"Any luck with that book?" he said, sitting down at a table next to Millicent.

"I think that stuff might be ectoplasm left from a phantasmal jellyfish."

Bostwick blinked. "Come again?"

"'Phantasmal jellyfish are a common pest found in Ataxia. They inhabit ancient structures such as castles, temples, and very old mansions. They are harmless, but annoying, trailing ectoplasm wherever they go. As the jellyfish are invisible, people often mistake their ectoplasm for strands of spider web, as they have very much the same sensation. This ectoplasm eventually falls to the ground, creating a sticky mess that can be removed by a solution of honey, egg yolks, and oil. Good luck cleaning that up afterwards.' That's what the book says, anyway. There's a picture, if you want to see."

"It's just a blank square," Bostwick said, peering at the book.

"I guess the author was trying to be funny."

"Well, at least we know how to get rid of it now. I don't suppose you have any honey or egg yolks with you?"

"No, but we can get some from the kitchen. We're almost done here anyway. You did a wonderful job. It would've taken me weeks to clean this place."

"Magic isn't just for show, you know."

"Oh, I know. I've read about all kinds of spells for things like fixing seams on clothing and buttoning shirts up all at once. I wish I could..." but she trailed off, then stood up. "Well, we should go to the kitchen. I can get you those ingredients before I make lunch."

Bostwick followed her out into the hallway down to a door with a sign saying *Kitchens* that opened onto a downward leading staircase. After descending for what must have been several floors, the stairs led into a cavernous earthen room with many tunnels leading off from it. This was filled with tables, cauldrons, and hanging spoons. Along the edge of the room were casks as big as elephants and row upon row of wooden drawers. Delilah stood next to one of the tables and brandished a large cleaver while speaking animatedly to Emmaline, who sat on the table.

"And if you use it this way," Delilah said, swinging the cleaver down onto the table, where it lodged in the wood, "you can chop right through the whole thing."

"Hi, Delilah," Millicent called. "Why are you chopping at the table?"

"I was just explaining about how we prepare pineapples."

"It's their national export," Emmaline added, trying to sound knowledgeable.

"Indeed, we alone among all the goblin countries have the means to grow the precious and much desired fruit. Although commonplace in your human society, pineapples are still a highly prized delicacy amongst our people."

"That's the reason they're so wealthy," Emmaline chimed in as if she was an expert on goblin economics, although she'd learned this all only a few minutes ago.

"Right you are," Delilah said approvingly. "Which is why the golden fruit adorns our flag, our architecture, and even our currency, the pin-a-pley."

"Fascinating," Bostwick said. "Now, where do you keep the honey and oil?"

"Humans sure do have a weird sense of taste," Delilah said.

"I'm not going to eat it. I'm cleaning with it."

"Cleaning is done for now! You must come learn about Styx!"

"What about lunch?" Millicent asked.

"No time for eating! We have edjification… efidication? Millicent, what's the word?"

"Why don't you stick with education?"

"That's boring, but it'll have to do."

"But the library is—" Before Bostwick could protest further, Delilah swept Emmaline up and led the whole group to yet another staircase that opened onto the hall of portraits.

"Let's see, we'll skip to the interesting ones. Ah, Bostwick, here's a face you should become familiar with."

She pointed to a picture of a tall goblin with an elaborately curled blue mustache. He wore military attire and was standing in front of a rack of clothes.

"This is Louis Fustian Jasper the Third, famous for making costumes and accessories. He invented the Domino of Nonpareil," she said matter-of-factly, but her eyes narrowed into a scowl, "and, boy if he knew a tricksy little human had gotten his slimy paws on it, he'd be spinning in his grave."

"Um, Delilah," Millicent began.

"Lucky for you," she continued with a smile, "he was cremated. Moving on."

She stopped in front of a large painting of a group of goblins surrounded by pineapple plants and orange trees. Some of the goblins were regally attired, while the rest were dressed quite sparingly, and one in the back looked like he might have been wearing nothing but a bath towel. Two figures stood out from this motley group. One was a tall goblin with a long braid of sea green hair running down his back. The other was a man with brown hair and a beard. The other figures in the painting sat as one would expect a person to pose for a portrait, well postured, looking at the artist. The two men, however, were turned to the side, engrossed by a small ball of light the green haired goblin held in his open hand, a mischievous grin on his face. Their strange pose, however, was not what caught Bostwick's attention. These two looked distinctly out of place from the rest of the group. The goblin, despite his pointy ears and snake eyes, could almost pass for a human. He would certainly be considered handsome by human standards, though he was slightly too feminine. The other man, although not particularly good looking, was definitely human.

"Who's that?" Bostwick asked, pointing to the man.

"Him?" Delilah said. "Oh, just a friend of the family."

"He's human."

"Yes. But so what? Millicent is human, and we're friends. Right, Millie?"

Millicent smiled and nodded.

"But why is he in this picture?" Bostwick continued.

"Because he was there at the time it was painted. Obviously."

"Why do I get the feeling there's something you aren't telling me?"

"I would never keep something from you, Bostwick! Unless it was for comedic effect, of course. Now, I show this painting because it commemorates a great day in Styx, three hundred years ago. Guess which one."

"Well," Emmaline began, "I guess all the people represent the different classes of goblins in Styx, and the pineapples represent wealth."

"The pineapples represent fruit," Delilah responded, "and everyone there is royalty except for the human."

"All of them? But there are so many. What happened?"

"We dwindled, you could say. Or rather we dispersed. Intermarriage between royalty is so unhealthy. Some of us went away to marry peasants of goblins elsewhere in Ataxia; some stayed to rule Styx and wed nobles from other countries. Speaking of which..."

She ran down the hall, leaving Bostwick and Emmaline to wonder about the significance of the group portrait. Delilah pointed up at a picture of two goblins.

"My parents!" she said proudly. "Raina Cacoethes Of Styx, and Bedlam Lesse."

Delilah's mother had bright green hair tied up in a spiky bun on the back of her head and green, triangular glasses, and had Delilah's father in a headlock under one arm. He had short, spiked, magenta hair and piercings all along his bat-like ears and one eyebrow. Both were smiling.

"Now I see where she gets it from," Bostwick mumbled under his breath, stopping at the portrait.

Emmaline stared hard at the picture and said, "They look... familiar, somehow."

Delilah snickered.

"Is that so? Well, my dear, I think it's time I told you—" but she was interrupted by a loud gong sounding outside.

"Darn, they stole my thunder!" Delilah said, heading down the hall to the green house.

"Well," said Bostwick, hurrying after Delilah, "that was far from 'edifying'."

"I'm more confused than before," Emmaline said.

"Don't be so whiny," Delilah commanded.

She reached the wall of glass behind the plants and threw open one of the window panes. Emmaline, who was still in Delilah's arms, looked down onto the front path outside the castle. A goblin with fur and cat-like whiskers was running up the path to the door.

"Hey, what do you want?" Delilah called down to it.

The goblin skidded to a halt and looked up.

"Your Majesty! There's been a bombing in town."

"What? Again?"

"This time it actually exploded. You must come quickly!"

"I'm coming, I'm coming. Was it at Heather's house again?

"Yes, Your Majesty."

"All right, tell 'em I'm coming."

Without waiting for a response, she shut the window and spun around to face Millicent and Bostwick.

"Well, that's annoying," she said to no one in particular.

"You are going, aren't you?" Emmaline asked, worried over the queen's lack of concern.

"Of course I am. I said I would. Besides, I have some shopping that needs doing. Come along, Bostwick."

"Why do I have to come?"

"Millicent will do the shopping," she replied, "and you'll carry all the heavy stuff. Besides, if you're going to be a proper butler, you're going to need to be acquainted with the townsfolk."

Three

A Bomb Scare?

Delilah led Emmaline and Bostwick to a small patio on the north side of the castle and walked over to a vine-covered ramada, under which was a large, lumpy object covered by a sheet. She whipped the sheet off with theatrical flare, revealing an open cart with two rows of seats facing outwards, away from each other, with one normal, forward-facing seat for the driver.

"What is that supposed to be?" Bostwick asked, unimpressed.

"This is a jaunty car. Magnificent, isn't it?"

"Ah-huh."

"You shall drive it."

"That's what I thought you'd say. Would it help if I told you I've never driven a carriage in my life?"

"You'll have to learn someday, what with being my chauffeur and all."

"I thought I was your butler."

"Yep, you're really moving up in the world. Now, Millicent should be around soon with the rodents."

"Rodents?" Emmaline asked. "I thought she went to get horses."

"Horses are too much upkeep. I much prefer giant capybaras."

Emmaline thought that perhaps the queen was joking, but sure enough, Millicent came from the garden leading two five-foot tall beasts that looked remarkably similar to guinea pigs with webbed feet. She hitched them up to the cart while Delilah floated up to one of the seats.

"You sit in front, Bostwick. That way you shall have a full view of where we're going."

"If you know so much, why don't you drive?"

"Don't be absurd. Who ever heard of a queen driving her own car?"

"Just use the reins," said Millicent, who sat on the side opposite Delilah, placing Emmaline on the seat beside her.

Bostwick gave the reins an experimental tug, but all that happened was that one of the capybaras turned his head around and grunted. He tried flicking the reins instead, but nothing happened. He looked at Millicent imploringly.

"Don't be troublesome, you two," she said to the rodents. "I know Bostwick is new at this, but if you give him a chance, I'm sure he'll get used to it. Please?"

The capybaras looked at each other, apparently making a decision, and started at a slow trot towards the castle gate that Bostwick and Emmaline had come through yesterday, which seemed a lifetime ago.

"So why aren't you driving?" Bostwick asked the maid.

"The capybaras won't let me. They say a lady shouldn't callous her hands. I don't mind, but they insist."

Bostwick said nothing, but wondered, briefly, if perhaps he was the only sane person left in the world.

"Ooh! Look at that amazing thing!" cried Delilah suddenly.

Bostwick turned around to look, but saw nothing out of the ordinary.

"Aw, you missed it by that much. Yikes! Keep your eyes on the road, would you?"

They soon came into a patch of forest, and the capybaras picked up speed. Delilah again yelled, "Look at that!"

"You're just being childish now," Bostwick complained.

"No, really, look, before it runs away."

Against his better judgment, Bostwick looked over his shoulder and, of course, saw nothing.

"You're easily distracted for a driver, aren't you? What if we hit something?"

"Then why don't you stop yelling for me to look at things that aren't there?"

"But that would take all the fun out of riding in a jaunty car!"

"Look out for that sea serpent!" Emmaline cried.

"Oh, don't you start," Bostwick said.

"No, look!"

Bostwick barely had time to turn back around and see a shining, scaly serpent writhing on the forest floor ahead of them. They would surely have flattened it if Millicent hadn't reached over and seized the reins just in time. The capybaras skidded to a halt and the cart lurched to a standstill behind them.

Millicent hopped down and ran to the serpent.

"The poor thing," she said, picking it up. It was easily twice as long as she was tall, but she seemed to have no trouble holding it. Bostwick picked Emmaline up and got down to inspect it.

"It's definitely from the ocean," said Emmaline. "See how it's got those fins and gills? I saw some of these when I vacationed in the Opal Islands."

"But what's it doing here?" asked Bostwick.

"Heather," came Delilah's reply.

"Who?"

"Heather Beatrice Monsters, the mapmaker we are going to see. I'm sure she's behind this."

"Her name is Heather B. Monsters and she makes maps?" Bostwick asked.

"Yes."

"Goblins…"

"Aren't we marvelously clever? Now, let's get back in the car and go see what Heather was thinking."

"We can take him with us, can't we?" Millicent asked.

"Of course. We can put him in the fountain in the town square."

They got back on the jaunty car and continued on. Millicent cradled the serpent like a baby in her arms as much as she could, but it was so long that Delilah held the tail, which she flicked back and forth for the rest of the journey.

When they arrived at the edge of town, the capybaras slowed down. The buildings were a mishmash of styles from every era, and most combined human and goblin elements. Many looked dilapidated and in danger of collapsing, but Bostwick knew from experience that goblins intentionally built things this way to appeal to chaotic aesthetics. Strange creatures ambled down the streets, some wearing starched suits and finely embroidered dresses, while others sported crudely sewn leather and rags. A few wore nothing at all, but their anatomy was so different from humans that it didn't matter anyway.

When they reached the town square, Delilah called for Bostwick to stop.

"Where should I park?" he asked.

"Just here, next to the fountain."

"But we're right in the middle of everything."

"I'm the queen; I can park anywhere I want."

Bostwick pulled back on the reigns to stop the car and the capybaras mercifully obeyed. Millicent got down and put the serpent in the fountain.

"All right," said Delilah. "We want to do things efficiently, so Emmaline and I will investigate the bomb threat. Millicent, you and Bostwick will shop. Here's a list."

She handed the maid a small folded paper, then picked Emmaline up. "You don't mind if I carry you on my head, do you?"

"No, of course not," the rabbit responded, curious why Delilah asked this time when she'd simply whisked her up like a hat this morning.

"Then we're off! Ta-ta, you two."

Bostwick watched her walk down one of the side streets, then asked Millicent, "So, what's on the list?"

"Just groceries. We can get most of it over here," she said, indicating an open market that took up much of the main street ahead.

♠ ♦ ♣ ♥ ♣ ♦ ♠

"So, we're going to meet Heather?" Emmaline asked, gazing at many colorful fruit stalls from her perch on Delilah's head.

"First, we must speak to the police."

"Police?"

"What, you find the idea odd?"

Emmaline adjusted herself to avoid slipping. They had just started down a stone stairway that led away from the market into a row of cobblestone and mortar houses.

"I never really pictured goblins having a police force. It seems so…"

"Lawful?"

"Yes."

"Hmm. We never used to have them, but one of my ancestors saw a human play which had the most amusing singing police, so we just had to have our own."

"Do they sing?"

"No. When the force was formed, it was voluntary, and the only people who wanted to join were a clan of Armored Bugbears from the Gammon Coast. Ironically, they used to be pirates."

Emmaline shifted again.

"And do they keep order, what with their… background?"

"Oh, don't worry. This generation is perfectly law abiding and mostly law enforcing. We haven't had to quell a rebellion since I was a child."

They continued on, taking a few side streets, and came to

a huge mound of earth. Sticking out of the mound were broken boards and snapped pipes.

"What happened here?" Emmaline asked.

"This is the police station. Why, what did you expect?"

Emmaline did not respond, but instead braced herself for what they might find inside.

They entered the station through a broken doorway. The interior was laid out like a human police station with several chairs, a front counter, and some desks behind that, except that everything—the walls, furniture, and floor—was constructed out of brick-a-brack. There were tarnished guns and knives, broken clocks, rotting wooden stools, and one shining, though twisted, candelabra. It was as though every piece of evidence that had ever been confiscated in Styx had been incorporated into the walls of the building. The windows, which were set here and there in the ceiling and walls, were grimy and blue. Emmaline was still looking around in wonder as Delilah walked up to the front counter, where several goblins were examining a wrench that was covered in an unsavory-looking red goo.

"Blood?" Delilah asked.

"Marinara sauce. Old and caked on, but maybe still edible. Evidence in a poisoning, you see," one of the goblins said.

Emmaline looked at the goblin, a bugbear Delilah had said, though there was more of bug than bear about him. He was about three feet in height and was very round, with a segmented blue shell on his back. His front was flat and fleshy, with no distinguishing features save for his eyes—which were small, black, and squinty—and a bushy mustache.

In Emmaline's mind, and probably everyone else who saw him, he resembled a large pill bug. So did the other two goblins with him, although they lacked mustaches. Before she could stop herself, she uttered, "Roly-polies."

"That's an intelligent hat you have there," the mustachioed bugbear said. "Yes, the Roly Police, finest lawmen in all of Ataxia, if I do say so myself."

"She's not a hat, actually," Delilah informed him. "She's a rabbit."

"A talking rabbit," one of the others said, "how odd. Hey, Folderol, get a load of this."

Folderol, who was also a bugbear, though much larger, turned and walked over to them. In his crustacean hands he held a long, frayed rope, which he placed on the counter.

"Talking rabbits are all well and good, but we've got work to do," he said, eyeing his colleagues with annoyance.

"Right," said the mustachioed bug. He pushed the wrench into the hands of the bugbear who hadn't spoken, who crawled up the wall and away down a hallway into parts unknown. Emmaline had no doubt that the vital piece of evidence would never be seen again. The remaining bugs picked up the rope and passed it from hand to hand.

"Anyway, Chief," Delilah asked, "I'm here about the bombing."

"Ah, yes. Well, it was at Heather's place, as was the last one, only this time, it went off."

"Any casualties?"

"No, but a few of Heather's maps were destroyed."

"No problem there," said Folderol. "She's probably already started re-drawing them."

"Anyway, we have the older bomb, if you want to see it."

"Yes, please," said the queen.

The large bugbear stomped away and returned a few moments later carrying a small metal sphere. He placed it on the counter for Delilah to inspect.

"So far as we know, this bomb is identical to the one that blew up today. We think it's the same perpetrator."

"Any profile?"

"We found some black hair at the scene, and judging by the engineering that went into this bomb, he didn't have any thumbs."

"You can tell that just by looking at it?" Emmaline asked.

"Sure we can. Let's be honest, it's not very well put together. That's probably why this one didn't blow up. It's hard to make an exploding mechanism without any thumbs," said the chief, rolling the sphere around on the counter. In mid-roll, he stopped.

"Do you hear that?"

It was a slow, mechanical clicking noise. Everyone leaned toward the device.

"It's coming from the bomb!"

"I thought you said it was a dud!" Emmaline cried.

"Well, I guess I set it off."

The ticking got faster and smoke started to spew from the screwed-together seams.

"It's gonna blow!"

All the police jumped and, in mid air, curled into tight balls. They would be protected by their thick shells, but Emmaline could not say the same for herself and Delilah.

"Aren't you going to get behind something?"

"But I want to see it blow up," Delilah said.

"You'll blow up too, you idiot!"

"Oh."

But it was too late. The ticking stopped, and the metal shell blew off in four pieces, one shooting right past Delilah's ear. Where the bomb had once been now lay a small, singed circle of mechanical parts and powder. Other than that, there was no damage.

"I must say I'm disappointed," said the queen, as the police unrolled from their shells. "Is this why Heather's still alive and well?"

"The other bomb had a bigger explosion, but not by much," said the chief.

"I think I've seen enough. If you find any more clues, send me a note."

"Will do."

"Where to now?" Emmaline asked, as they left the station.

"We shall pay a visit to Heather. Ask her if she saw anything unusual."

I don't think anything in Styx can be called usual, Emmaline mused to herself.

"So what's next?" Bostwick asked, adjusting his grip on the grocery sack. So far, it was filled with brightly colored and strange smelling vegetables and a package of meat.

"Let's see," Millicent replied, examining the list, "all that's left is some mushrooms. There should be a stall selling them over here."

"What exactly is this food for, anyway?"

"Bat-mushroom stew."

Bostwick halted in place.

"Then this meat is…?"

"Bat."

He grimaced.

"It's not half as bad as it sounds."

"It's still pretty horrible, then?"

"When all the ingredients are combined, and spices are added, you'd never know it was bat. I promise."

Bostwick reluctantly followed her to the next stall. Dried mushrooms hung from the ceiling and fresh ones occupied shelves all around. Millicent inspected them, as Bostwick had no clue what would make one mushroom better than another. When she had purchased a single mushroom cap that was as wide as a dinner plate, they made their way back to the jaunty car. The capybaras were nowhere in sight.

"They're probably at the pub," Millicent said.

"Well, shouldn't they be coming back soon?" Bostwick said, wondering what, exactly, capybaras would be doing at a pub.

"Delilah's not back yet, so it's all right. We can just wait here for her, I guess."

Wait they did, for several minutes. Bostwick occupied the time thinking of ways to give Delilah the slip without being cursed. Millicent simply stared into space, while glancing at Bostwick every so often. As the time went on her looks toward him became more and more frequent, and thus increasingly annoying.

"Something on your mind?" he asked.

"Oh, I was just thinking, or wondering, I suppose, what was it like at Melieh's Academy?"

"It was all right," he said shortly.

"Was it good to be around so many other magicians? I mean, do you think that helped you learn magic better?"

"Not really."

"What do you mean? Didn't you like it there?"

"I liked the school, just not all the people. Magicians have a tendency to be really stuck up and competitive."

"How come?"

"Don't ask me. Everyone just thought they were so amazing for getting into the Academy, like they were the elite or something, when really, as long as you can do magic, they'll accept you."

"And if you pass the personality test."

"Well, that too, but... Wait, how do you know about the test?"

"I read about it," she said quickly. A little too quickly, Bostwick thought.

"Yeah, they have to make sure you aren't going to use your magic to do terrible, evil things. But no one fails that test."

"But you said everyone was all pompous."

"Pomposity isn't the same thing as evil. It's just..."

He would have stopped talking, but Millicent seemed to be genuinely interested in the situation. Also, he felt like there was something she wasn't telling him, and he wanted to know what it was.

"Well," he began, "most of the students at the Academy are somewhat upper class, but that's just because people from lower class families actually have to work for a living and can't spend all that time at school. So magicians from the lower class were somewhat rare, like me. Plus there's the stigma associated with being a von Dogsbody."

"Stigma?" Millicent asked.

Bostwick sighed.

"Even though my parents are shop keepers, they're still members of the von Dogsbody family, which is famous for producing some of the most skilled servants in the Empire. They're specialists at whatever they do, from gardening to cooking to whatever else. If you have a von Dogsbody working for you, it's pretty prestigious, and plenty of my classmates' families employed von Dogsbodies. So for them to go to school with someone who would normally be doing their laundry or serving them dinner was a little awkward.

"It didn't really matter too much at first. After all, there were a few other students from lower class families, but then, well, I caught on faster than the rest of them, I guess."

"Didn't you say you were first in your class?"

"I was. The Academy even let me graduate a year early since I had mastered almost every spell in my first three years," Bostwick said, a bit self-consciously. "But some other students couldn't stand that. They always tried to outdo me, but they couldn't. At least, until the last semester, when we learned the art of Rabbit Conjuration."

"Oh, dear."

"I couldn't do it. And suddenly, everyone got the idea that that made me inferior to them. Even the students who were barely passing thought that they'd somehow beat me at my own game."

"That's awful! It doesn't sound like the Academy is very nice at all."

"It wasn't all bad. To tell the truth, watching everyone else try the hat trick was pretty entertaining. Some people pulled out dead rabbits, or rabbits with mange. And my roommate tried to pull a jackalope out of a fez. The antlers got stuck, of course."

"Oh my! It didn't get hurt, did it?"

"No, no. Actually, when he did get it out, he kept it as a pet. I suppose there was one good person there."

"Hmm?"

"My roommate, Clarence. He's actually related to the empress, but that didn't go to his head. He was just happy to be doing any magic, no matter how badly. He actually *wanted* to be a door-to-door magician, so he could see the world. I'd trade lives with him in a heartbeat."

"Are you really unhappy here, Bostwick?"

"Of course. Aren't you?"

Millicent looked her feet. "Well, I'm tired of waiting, if that's what you mean."

"Bored?" came a shrill voice from out of nowhere. Bostwick and Millicent looked around, but there was no one to be seen, until a small, pointed, whiskery face poked out from under the cart.

"If you're bored," the creature said, "why not try our antique shop? It's full of lovely things to interest two humans such as yourselves."

"I love antiques!" Millicent said, hopping onto the ground and crouching to be at eye level with the face.

"I thought you might! You're the queen's maid, aren't

you? I've heard about you from a friend of a friend. Yes, I think you will very much like our antiques. Did I mention some of them are magical?"

Millicent stood up, practically jumping off the ground as she did so. "Let's go, Bostwick. Delilah won't mind. We can just leave a note telling her where we went."

"Fine by me," Bostwick said. If there really were magical items at the shop, it could be his best chance for curing Emmaline or escaping Delilah's clutches unscathed.

While Millicent wrote the note, the goblin crawled out from under the cart. It was short and furry, with a long bald tail and scythe-like claws. When it stood upright, Bostwick saw that it was actually wearing a three-piece suit.

"Ah, but I've forgotten to introduce myself," the goblin said. "I am Jigory Tripe, owner and proprietor of the Rare and Priceless Antique Shop."

Several blocks from the police station was a quaint yellow house with a trim, civilized garden. Over the porch hung a sign with painted letters reading, simply, *Cartographer*. Delilah hopped up the two steps that led onto the porch, jostling Emmaline, and knocked on the door. After a few moments, she knocked again, more firmly. Still, no one answered.

"Maybe she's out," Emmaline offered.

"Not likely." Delilah tapped her foot impatiently, then began to pound on the door with all her might. "It's Delilah, you hear! Open up or so help me, I'll—"

Emmaline never found out what the queen would have done, for the door opened and a goblin stuck her head out to inspect her visitors. She had brown hair on her head, pulled back into a loose, messy bun, and the rest of her body was covered with light brown fur.

"Oh, it's you," she said, barely pausing between words. "Yes, do come in. Of course, of course."

The inside of the house was actually one large room, with one corner separated by a folding screen. The only furniture was a low table in the very center of the room; the rest of the floor was taken up by rolls of paper and bottles of ink, and the walls were covered haphazardly with maps of various places in Ataxia.. As Emmaline looked around, she noticed that some of the maps were scorched and damaged, no doubt from the bombing that had happened that morning.

"Watch your step," Heather said, sliding her feet along the floor to avoid crushing anything.

Delilah apparently thought this far too much trouble and floated above the debris over to the table, where she and Emmaline sat down just as Heather made it there on foot.

"Well, what d'ya think?" Heather asked, gesturing to the tabletop where a map of Styx was rolled open. "It's not done yet, of course, but so far so good, yeah?"

"Actually, I came to ask about the bombing."

"Of course; that's all anyone worries about any more. No one cares about maps in this day and age. What's the world coming to?"

She pulled a handkerchief out of her pocket with her long, furry tail and blew her pointy nose.

"Don't be like that, Heather. I care about your maps very much, which is why I don't want them blown to pieces. Now, did you see the bomber?"

"All I know is, I left the shop for not five minutes to get some lovely hot beverage, and when I came back, my beautiful maps were in burnt little pieces all over the floor!"

"That was fast. What about yesterday? You didn't see anyone then, either?"

"No. That time the bomb was there when I woke up, ticking and all, but it just stopped on its own."

"Hmm. This guy's clever, whoever he is."

"Anyway," said Heather, "now that we've established I know nothing about this bomber, let's talk about something I do know."

Delilah and Emmaline looked back to the map. It was not finished by anyone's standards, and now Emmaline knew who had drawn the map of the castle. This map, too, was stained and scribbled, with many of the place names jammed close together so it was almost impossible to tell what was where. Emmaline looked at the town, then followed a winding line that must have been the road leading up to the castle. Then something caught her eye. Next to the road, a serpent was drawn, in the same way a sea monster would be drawn on the ocean of a regular map. Above the serpent's head, a question mark was written.

"How did you know about this?" Emmaline asked the mapmaker, who screamed.

"A talking rabbit! What on earth?"

"Oh, this is my new guest, Heather," Delilah said. "Allow me to introduce Emmaline Camellia. Don't be rude, answer her question."

"Oh, uh, the serpent? I just drew that to see what would happen if I put a sea serpent on land."

"I thought that was you. Well, it really showed up. Proud of yourself?"

"Wait," said Emmaline, putting two and two together. "You mean you drew the serpent, and it actually appeared where you drew it?"

"Of course," Heather replied. "The official mapmakers of Styx have a very special ability. The landscape of Styx changes to however we draw it on our map. Pretty amazing, eh?"

"But don't you realize what this means?" Emmaline asked. "The bomber, whoever he was, wasn't just trying to blow up your maps, he was trying to destroy Styx!"

Delilah and Heather glanced at each other, unfazed.

"Well, obviously that's what they were going for," Heather said, "but really they just succeeded in making a mess, and making my life a lot harder."

"But how can you be so unconcerned, especially you, Delilah? Your people's lives are in danger."

"Hmph, yeah right," the queen said, tossing her hair out of her face. "This bomber's just an ignorant fool, Emmaline. As everyone knows, only the true ruler of Styx can permanently damage the map. If anyone else tries, things will just stay the same until Heather draws another version."

"So the bomber thought wrong," said Emmaline, "but even so, there's someone out there who wants to destroy Styx! Delilah, do you have any enemies?"

"Well, not personally, but every goblin who isn't Styxian himself, and even a few who are, wouldn't mind blowing us up. Goblins have a taste for trouble, as I'm sure you're aware," she said, fiddling with Emmaline's rabbit ears to drive the point home.

Frustrated with the queen's lack of concern, Emmaline hopped to the floor and started crawling under maps, sniffing for clues.

"You're wasting your time," Delilah said. "The police have already swept the area, remember? Besides, I'm sure whoever it was will realize their mistake and stop bombing this place."

"What if they don't? What if they try to find another way to destroy the country?"

Delilah shrugged and rolled up the map, then scooped Emmaline off the floor.

"In the event of an all-out attack on Styx, the Roly Police will deal with it. And if they fail, then I can whip out some old Styx magic. But I'm sure it won't come to that," the queen said, as if it were written in stone.

Four

Rare and Priceless Counterfeits

Jigory led Bostwick and Millicent down several winding streets and up an alley where a number of unsavory-looking merchants sat hawking their wares. Though Bostwick felt that all goblins were fairly unscrupulous, these seemed especially so, giving him the feeling that they had somehow stumbled into the seedy part of town. The products here included many more body parts than in the main street market had, and one scaly goblin even offered to sell them what he referred to as a "slightly used heart," though Bostwick thought it looked more like a yam. Thankfully, Jigory kept most of the merchants at bay by swiping at them with his claws.

He finally stopped in front of a large, open front shop and led them inside. Antiques covered every square inch of the store, leaving only a narrow path for customers to walk down.

"Well," Jigory said, hopping onto an ancient umbrella stand, which rocked precariously underneath him, "I'll just let you look around. Don't mind me."

With that, he scrambled up a grandfather clock behind him and swiftly disappeared.

"This is so exciting," Millicent said. "I didn't know there was a store like this in Styx. I hope we find something magical."

"This stuff looks pretty ordinary to me," Bostwick said, examining an intricately carved wardrobe. "Even if it is 'rare and priceless', who cares about rare and priceless furniture?"

"Maybe it's enchanted furniture. I've heard of things like that. Let's see what the tag says."

She grabbed the paper tag hanging from the wardrobe and read aloud. "'The famed Fuchsia Wardrobe of Queen Bellicosity of Gammon. Said to turn any garment placed within a violent shade of pink.' See, it *is* magic."

Bostwick, skeptical to the last, took out a white handkerchief and placed it in the wardrobe. He shut the door, then opened it again to find the handkerchief unchanged.

"Maybe there are instructions," Millicent said, flipping the tag over. "Oh, it just says the name of the store."

"I knew it. I bet everything in here is a fake."

"Well, it's still pretty," Millicent said, dropping the tag. "Besides, they probably keep the magic things in a different part of the store."

Bostwick doubted this, but he followed her through the rest of the antiques.

Delilah and Emmaline, meanwhile, were making their way back to the jaunty car, though Delilah insisted on meandering through the market on their way there. Emmaline didn't know what they where looking for until Delilah stopped before a small purple tent.

"What have we here? We must go inside, Emmaline."

"Why? I thought Bostwick was going to do the shopping."

"Yes, but this shop is purple, and purple is my favorite color. Which must mean they have something simply splendid within! Understand?"

"Not really."

The queen simply gave a purr-like chuckle and entered the shop.

They were met with a very dark interior where a number of jars and bottles of colorful liquids filled the shelves. There was also a counter with a purple tablecloth, which took up a large portion of the space.

"And what do you sell here, sir?" Delilah asked. Emmaline wondered whom she was speaking to, until she saw movement behind the counter. A man, who had previously been facing away from them, turned swiftly around. He wore a black cloak, which was why he'd been so difficult to see in the dim light, with a hood over his head so that they couldn't see his eyes. In fact, no part of his body but his long, thin hands—blackish blue in color—and his wide smile were distinguishable.

"What do I sell? Why, memories, of course!" he said, in an exuberantly salesman-like way.

"Ah, I could use a new one of those," Delilah said thoughtfully.

"I'm afraid you don't understand. I sell *memories*, not memory."

"I see! Well, that's even better."

"I don't see the difference," Emmaline interjected.

The shopkeeper started, but Delilah cut across his shock.

"Yes, she's a talking rabbit. Moving on."

"Oh, yes, well, the difference between memory and memories is, well…" he hunched over the counter and held his head in one hand, thinking. "Hmm, I suppose it's like the difference between a *bad* memory and a bad *memory*."

"Yes, that makes perfect sense," Delilah said, joining him in leaning on the counter.

"I don't see how," Emmaline complained.

"Memory is everything you remember," Delilah said. "They are your own; whereas *memories* are each *a thing* remembered, and can sometimes be shared by people. It's a bit like vision versus a particular sight."

"Exactly!" The shopkeeper said, although Emmaline was still rather confused. "I sell the second kind of memory. Care for a sample?"

He took a delicate glass bottle off the shelf behind him and passed it to Delilah, who gazed at it, perplexed.

"So, do I… do I drink it?"

"I wouldn't advise it. You smell it, of course."

"Oh," she said, and sniffed the glass stopper. Without warning, she jumped up, held one hand in the air, and began to gesture wildly as she spoke. "Of course, I remember it now! I was walking through a field of daffodils and it was beginning to rain. I ran down a grassy hill, thoroughly soaking my dress on the dew, and I… I…" but she stopped, looking down at the shopkeeper. "Where's the rest? What happens next?"

"That was just a sample. For a more complete memory, you need the whole bottle."

"How much does it cost?"

"All of these," he pulled a plum colored basket filled with an assortment of atomizers from below the counter, "are only ten pin-a-pleys. But this offer is open today only. Tomorrow is too late! Plus, as a special offer to royalty only, I'll throw in a bonus item for free!"

"Ooh! What's the bonus?"

The shopkeeper's smile faltered.

"You know, I hadn't really thought that far ahead. Is there anything in particular you want?"

"Hmm… I've got it! I want you to tell me the secret behind making memories."

"Delilah!" Emmaline said sternly. "You can't ask someone to tell you the secret of their livelihood. If it got out, anyone could make memories. He'd be out of a job."

"Oh, hush." She turned back to the shopkeeper and smiled as innocently as a goblin could. "Don't worry. Your secret's safe with me."

The man looked at the basket of memories, apparently deliberating how much they were worth.

"Well…" he finally said, "making memories can be done by two methods. First, you can simply fabricate one by combining the proper ingredients required for retention with the desired scent."

"Scent?" Emmaline asked.

"Memories are based largely on smell. You could say that's their main ingredient. The rest is just the medium they move through. Anyway, as I said, they can be made artificially. The second way… well, it's a lot more dangerous."

"Ooh, do go on!" Delilah implored.

"It's possible to collect a person's memory, but it's a very complicated process. First, you have to have these."

He took a large jar from the back wall and held it up for Delilah to see. The jar was filled with dried, white herbs.

"These are daft stocks collected straight from the Plains of Umber. As they are now, they're useless, but when put into the open air, they absorb surrounding scents and, along with them, memories. These can then be steeped in a concoction that will allow those who didn't have the memory to experience it. But the person who you took the memory from originally will have absolutely no recollection of the events that occurred while they were in contact with the herbs. For this reason, memory collection is rarely used as a—"

"I wanna try it!"

"What? But Y-Your Majesty, I just said it comes with a terrible price!"

"Oh, what's one or two memories here or there going to cost me? I've forgotten so much already that it probably won't make any difference."

"But it's not only that! Memory collection is an inexact science. It's difficult to pinpoint when the herbs will start absorbing and when they stop. Also, the memories have to be fresh. If you try to leach out old memories, disastrous consequences will ensue!"

Delilah raised an eyebrow.

"I want to try it."

"I-it's far too dangerous and unpredictable. It would be irresponsible—"

The queen narrowed her eyes.

"I won't buy anything unless you give me at least enough

herbs to make one memory."

Having no choice, the shopkeeper scooped a teaspoon of herbs into a small satchel and put it in a jar. Handing the jar to Delilah he said, "Don't open this until you want to start absorbing memories. Close it up again as soon as you're done. And please, whatever you do, keep it short and simple."

"Of course. And how am I to make it back into a smellable recollection?"

"The process is complicated. I'll write it down for you so you don't... forget."

As he scribbled instructions on a long piece of paper, Delilah produced a wallet, seemingly out of nowhere, and pulled out ten large yellow coins.

"See, Emmaline? I told you this shop would have something interesting inside."

Millicent seemed enthralled by everything she walked past, and would have gladly examined each antique for hours had Bostwick not insisted on moving on. He, so far, had found nothing of interest.

"Ooh, what about this?" Millicent said, picking up a translucent pink rock. "The tag says 'wishing stone.' Do you think it really grants wishes?"

"It might, if it were real," he said, examining the stone. "It's probably a fake."

"But the sign says it's rare and priceless."

"It may be rare and priceless, but it's still a fake, just like everything else here."

He replaced the stone and continued on, but Millicent stared at it for a while longer before joining him.

Gradually, they made their way towards the back of the shop. The items here were even stranger than those at the front, and a great deal more dangerous. There were bottles marked *Poison* and vials that had the word *Poison* crossed off and replaced with *Harmless water. Do have some.* There were lumpy objects covered in fur, busts of famous monarchs and not-so-famous bartenders, as well as a series of dangerous-looking weapons, the most intimidating of which was a device with spikes and blades jutting out at every angle, but without any sort of handle. And, of course, everything was marked *Rare and Priceless*.

"Bostwick," Millicent began as she sorted through portraits of livestock, "what if that stone was real? What would you wish for?"

"To not be a prisoner of that mad queen of yours," he said without missing a beat.

"Oh."

"Why? What would you wish for?"

Her face suddenly became transported, like she was in a completely different place than a dark and somewhat damp antique shop. "I would wish to sit under a tree next to a river on an overcast day and have a picnic in the shade with my very best friends. I have a lovely vision of me wearing a bright yellow sundress. We would eat sandwiches and potato salad, and enjoy each other's company."

Bostwick stared at her with out saying a word, his expression completely unreadable. Millicent had never seen such an intense stare; it made her blush. For lots of reasons.

"W-what?"

He hesitated and then said, "That's dumb."

Millicent's lovely vision shattered into a thousand shining pieces.

"What's wrong with it?"

"Well, it's so simple, so mundane. You shouldn't waste wishes on that sort of thing."

"Oh," she said, slumping her shoulders.

"Hey, don't get like that. If you want a wish like that, it's fine. Don't let me tell you what to wish for."

"Mmm."

"And don't do that 'mmm' thing. If you have something to tell somebody, tell them."

Millicent raised her head, paused, then said, "A cat!"

"What?"

"There's a cat over there on that shelf! Look!"

"Yeah, I see it, but weren't we talking about wishes?"

Millicent had clearly forgotten about wishes for the moment. She rushed over to the corner of the store, where a large black and white cat sat on the highest shelf, staring down at them.

"It's so cute! Come here, kitty," she said, trying to coax it down.

The cat obeyed, leaping off the shelf and hitting the floor with a thud, then looked up at them. It certainly looked soft and fluffy, but Bostwick could not see the creature as cute.

"It's kind of creepy, isn't it?" he said.

"That's a terrible thing to say!"

"But look at its face. It's so blank and expressionless, almost inhuman."

"It's a cat, though," Millicent said with a laugh.

"But even cats have personality. It looks more like a person pretending to be a cat, and not doing a very good job of it."

"That's very astute of you," it said.

Millicent let out a small "eek!" but Bostwick, who was used to talking animals, said, "So what exactly are you, then?"

"That's the question, isn't it?" the cat said. Now it had an expression, and not one that Bostwick cared for in the least. Its yellow eyes were narrowed into a glare and the edges of its mouth rose ever so slightly into a smile.

"Whatever," said Bostwick, not caring to know anything else about the animal. He went back to looking through dusty items.

Millicent was mesmerized by the beast, not because it could talk, but because it looked tremendously huggable. She reached down to pet its head, but it twisted away and swiped her hand with its claws.

"Ow! I wasn't going to hurt you."

The cat retreated several feet, losing its stand-offish demeanor.

"I'm sorry," it said, bowing its head. "I'm not used to being touched. Did *I* hurt *you?*"

"It's just a little scratch. I should have asked permission, I guess."

"But it's bleeding," the cat said, concern edging into its voice.

"Let me see," said Bostwick, reentering the conversation.

Millicent held out her hand, which had open cuts across two fingers.

"We need a box," Bostwick said, looking around the shop. He grabbed a small box filled with buttons from one of the shelves and dumped its contents onto the floor, then took Millicent's hand, put it into the open end, and moved his hands several times over the box in motions that were too fast for Millicent to make out clearly. When he removed the box, her fingers were healed.

"How'd you do that?" she asked, inspecting her hand.

"It's a variation on sawing a woman in half. You can't very well cut people in half if you don't close up the wound. That would just be disgusting."

"I never thought of that."

"You," said a voice from the floor, "you're a magician!"

"Of course," said Bostwick to the cat.

"But what are you doing here of all places?"

"If you mean in this shop, we're just killing time. But I'm in Styx because of your queen."

"She is not my queen!" the cat spat. "And if you were smart you would have nothing to do with her, either."

"I would leave if I could, but I'll be cursed if I don't work for her, so…"

"You work for her?" the cat said curiously.

"Only until I figure out a way to escape without getting cursed too badly."

"That's not wise. The curses of the goblins of Styx are formidable and, so far as I can tell, unbreakable."

"Let me guess, you have personal experience with them?"

The cat paused, sighed, and then spoke.

"I wasn't always a cat. But the Styx goblins saw fit to trap me in this pathetic form, and I have yet to find a way to change myself back."

"Just how many people has Delilah trapped, anyway?"

"Her family's accursed influence has spread too far to measure. "

"Stop it!" Millicent cried, causing both the cat and Bostwick to jump. "Listen," she continued more quietly, "I'm sorry that you got turned into a cat, but Delilah certainly didn't do it."

"No, she wasn't the one who cursed me, it's true, but she's just as terrible as the rest of her people. The Styx goblins have a long history of ruining people's lives."

"Well, Delilah didn't ruin my life," Millicent said, incensed. "She's my friend and I refuse to hear anything else insulting said about her."

"Very well, then," the cat said. "I'll leave you with this warning. The Styx goblins are not what they seem. Don't let yourself be fooled by them. They may seem sophisticated and altruistic, almost human, but nothing could be further from the truth."

He leapt back up onto his shelf and walked along to an open window.

"See you around, magician," he said, disappearing.

"I don't think anyone has ever thought of the Styx goblins as altruistic," Bostwick said.

"Oh, I wouldn't say that," said Jigory, who popped out of a pile of clothing that sat nearby. "The queen was nice enough to let us open up shop here. She's such a wise, kind, wonderful ruler."

"There's nothing wonderful about allowing a charlatan to sell forgeries to the unsuspecting masses."

"Charlatan! Why, sir, you have cut me to the quick. Surely, each item here is a work of art."

"They're all worthless copies."

"Copies, yes, but worthless, absolutely not."

"Then they really aren't real after all?" Millicent asked, sounding crushed.

"Of course not. This is the Rare and Priceless Counterfeit Shop; we never sell originals."

"You said it was an antique shop."

"Did I? Ah, yes, so I did. But you never would have come if you thought it was all counterfeit. You had to see it."

"Seeing it now," Bostwick said, "I wouldn't have come anyway."

"You aren't impressed? That's a shame. But I'm sure if you spoke to the artist, perhaps you'd change your mind."

"The artist?" Millicent asked. "You mean one person made all this? That's amazing."

"She'll be glad to hear that," Jigory said, looking around. "Now, if we can just find her... Ah, of course."

He scurried over to a large vase and tipped it over sideways, revealing another goblin curled up inside, fast asleep. This goblin looked indistinguishable from Jigory, except that the ends of her whiskers were curled.

"Polk," Jigory said, shaking the vase from side to side. "Polk, wake up. We've got customers."

"Customers?" she said sleepily.

"They say your stuff's amazing."

Polk's head shot up and she looked around, alert. She crawled out of the vase, stood up, and bowed in one fluid motion.

"Allow me to introduce my cousin, Polkory Tripe."

"Pleased to meetcha." Polk said. "So you really think I'm amazing, huh?"

"I think what Millicent meant was that the sheer volume of forgeries that you've made is impressive," Bostwick said with disdain in his voice.

"Please, let's call them counterfeits. It sounds so much nicer. So, are you interested in magical artifacts, or perhaps a rare painting?"

"We aren't interested in anything that isn't real."

"Real? Piffle, who cares if it's real? What matters is that it's true and beautiful and heartfelt. I only copy the best, but I still think my copies are better. Anyone can make a mythical item or paint a beautiful picture, but it takes a true artist, nay, a genius, to produce a counterfeit that can be mistaken for real."

She reached behind her and produced two identical paintings of a pineapple to illustrate her point. She studied each picture in turn, gave the left one a sniff, then the right, and finally shrugged. "Even I can't tell them apart."

"That may be true as far as artwork goes," Bostwick said, "but your magical items are a dead giveaway. They don't have the powers of the originals."

"Well, no, but that doesn't mean they don't have power. Take, for example, this," she said, snatching a red cloak off a hook on the wall. "This is a replica of the Legendary Cloak of Teleportation."

"The one that allows the wearer to transport anywhere in the world?" Bostwick asked.

"Indeed!"

"So what does this one do?"

"The cloak itself teleports anywhere in the world, without taking you with it. And this bag here—the original was said to be able to hold a thousand pounds and not break. But this one can hold twenty-five pounds and it feels as if it's empty."

"That could be useful," Millicent said.

"Not compared to the real one," said Bostwick.

"Well, it sounds silly when you compare it to the original, but on its own, I think it's really something special."

"You've obviously got good taste," Polk said, "if you think I'm amazing. I'm sure you've also got enough sense to buy something, because these works of art are selling fast!"

Bostwick was certain that last part was a complete lie, but before he could say anything, Millicent produced the wishing stone from behind her back and asked the price.

"You're actually buying that thing?" Bostwick asked skeptically

"A fine choice, my lady," Jigory said. "That will be thirty standard pin-a-pleys."

"I'm no expert on goblin currency," said Bostwick, "but that sounds like highway robbery."

"Are you paying for this?" Polk asked.

"Well, no."

"Then it doesn't matter how much we charge, so be quiet."

Millicent pulled out three yellow coins that were about the size of the coins from the Empire, and then two extremely wide coins that looked like they were made of the exact same metal. Bostwick was secretly relieved that he wasn't buying anything, because goblin currency confused him no end. Millicent handed the coins to Jigory, who scurried away between stacks of counterfeits, and Polk lead them out of the shop.

"Take good care of that stone," she said, "and come again soon."

Bostwick started to go, but Millicent turned back to Polk.

"I forgot to ask. Does this stone grant lots of wishes, or just one?"

"You know, I never tested it. I guess you should try it out and see. I can tell you this much: like the original version, when all of its power is exhausted, it should turn from pink to a dark green-black-peacock-type color."

"Thanks," Millicent said, waving goodbye.

On their way out of the alley, they were once again accosted by street vendors, but they walked fast enough to avoid conversation with any of them. When they finally made it back to the carriage, Emmaline, Delilah, and the capybaras were waiting for them.

"So you finally decided to show up, did you?" Delilah said. "We've been waiting for hours."

"Actually," Emmaline corrected, "we got here a few minutes ago."

"Delilah, we found the most incredible shop!" Millicent said. "It's called Rare and Priceless Counterfeits and everything there is made by one goblin, all by herself!"

"Yes, I know of that place," Delilah said. "A friend of a friend told me about how a counterfeit artisan and her cousin were looking for a place to open for business, and I simply had to have them in my town. You'll have to tell me all the details of your excursion on the ride home."

"I will, but first…" Millicent held out the stone. "I got this for you, Emmaline. It's supposed to be a wishing stone. I don't know if it'll work or not, but I figured you could try wishing to be human again."

"That's why you bought it?" Bostwick asked, looking slightly stunned.

Millicent nodded and placed the stone on the seat next to Emmaline.

"Thank you, Millicent," Emmaline said, clearly touched by the maid's kindness. She placed a paw on the stone and said, "I wish I could turn back into my human shape."

The stone neither glowed nor changed color, and Emmaline remained a rabbit.

Millicent looked downcast, but Delilah put her arm on the maid's shoulder, saying, "Well, who knows, maybe it'll just take a while. It's not the real thing, after all; we can't expect it to work perfectly."

They boarded the jaunty car and began their journey back to the castle. Millicent told Delilah about the antique shop, but without much heart. Bostwick added nothing to her account and simply drove forward, lost in thought. Millicent finished her story as they crossed through the castle gate.

"I'm sorry the stone didn't work," Millicent said at last.

"It's all right. At least you tried," Emmaline said.

"I just feel like the whole day was a complete waste," she said, getting slowly down from the cart.

"No," Delilah said to the maid, though her eyes were on Bostwick, who glanced back at Millicent as he carried Emmaline into the castle. "I think we've accomplished quite enough, for one day at least."

Five

Garden Variety Wyrms

The next three weeks passed uneventfully at Castle Styx. Though Bostwick still wanted to find some means of turning Emmaline human again, he had to spend most of his time doing various chores around the castle under threat of being cursed. It was up to the princess to find her own cure, so she started by exploring the building to see just what types of magical artifacts a goblin castle might hold. So far, she had found twenty-three bedrooms, four washrooms, two separate libraries (the one for cookbooks and the other for everything else), and a ballroom. Many of the rooms were connected by secret passages or exterior walkways, while others had very small doors or could only be accessed from a window. Some of the things she came across were quite curious, such as the card hallway, which she discovered curved gradually to the right until it made a complete spiral and ended at a hall closet. She peeked into a room marked *Treasure Chamber*, and found it filled with strange artifacts, such as glass armor, a huge crown that must have once belonged to a giant, and a long sword with a blade of black metal. Unfortunately, none of the treasure would help her get her human body back. She found another room with bare walls and no windows that seemed completely empty, until she looked up to see the ceiling was covered in glowing, upside-down flowers, but when she asked Delilah about their purpose, was told that they simply let the sunlight in.

Strangest of all, Emmaline thought, was that some rooms were spotless while others were in far worse condition than the library had been. She suspected that the maid had been cleaning the entire castle by herself for who knew how many years, and had not even gotten to some rooms yet. She wondered if Millicent was also a prisoner here. The girl didn't seem unhappy, and she and Delilah seemed to be on friendly terms. Often, when Bostwick was busy washing floors and dusting, Emmaline saw Millicent and the queen having tea or looking over stacks of voluminous books. And now, as Emmaline perused the lowest shelves in the upstairs library to see if any titles mentioned curses, Millicent presented her with a small, glitter-covered invitation.

"A sleepover?" Emmaline asked.

"Yes."

"But, don't we already live in the castle together?"

"Aha!" cried Delilah, as she stepped out from behind one of the bookcases. "But this is a special sleepover in my tower. Being high up is much better than being down low, as every goblin knows. I offer you this invitation as a sign of good will between Styx and Camellia."

"And suppose I didn't feel like staying up all night with you in your tower?"

"I would declare war on your puny principality and hold you for ransom. But that's such a silly question, because of course you'll accept.

"Of course," Emmaline said, a little fearfully.

That evening, when Emmaline arrived in Delilah's room, the queen insisted she wear the Domino because "what fun would a sleepover be as a rabbit?"

"I've set Bostwick to get us hot cocoa," Delilah said, "but in the meantime, how about this?" She held out a pink tin of tea with a picture of a seven-petaled flower on it.

"That's from Camellia!" Emmaline said, taking the tin with her now human hands. It was the first sign of home she'd seen in over a year. She blinked back a tear.

"I was just telling Millie how it's your main export. They have a bureau to ensure the highest quality leaves are used, and a tea inspector and everything."

"It's delicious," Millicent said. "We always have this kind of tea."

"Yes, goblin teas are a little… Well, we don't use the very best plants, you see, so I import human varieties. But on to a more important subject," she said, pouring tea into a strange, claw-footed cup and offering it to Emmaline. "We know all about Bostwick, but not so much about you. Especially this curse—how ever did it happen?"

"Very unexpectedly," Emmaline said, putting the tin down as she recalled a more unpleasant memory of home. "I was walking through our garden, when I stepped on some sort of long tail."

"All by itself?" Millicent asked.

"No, but not belonging to anything I could see. It was

very long, so I followed it into some bushes, and all of a sudden a goblin sprang up and snapped his fingers. The next thing I knew, I was a rabbit, and the goblin ran off."

"I wonder…" Delilah said, touching Emmaline's forehead briefly. "Nope. If that goblin had been at all related to me, that curse would have come right off and the Domino would show up."

"Is that the only way to undo a curse? To have someone in his family break it?"

"Oh, not the only way, but probably the most effective. Hmm," Delilah purred. "Though I applaud your decision to search for a cure to a goblin curse in a continent full of goblins, why on earth did you and Bostwick come alone?"

"If we took a royal entourage, it would have attracted too much attention. I'm fairly sure that if any goblins knew I was a princess, they would certainly have kidnapped me. I've been told they enjoy creating international incidents."

"Of course," the queen replied, though Emmaline couldn't tell if she was agreeing that the lack of entourage made sense or that international incidents were fun, "but if that's the case, why bring Bostwick at all?"

"He was the only one with any magical training that we knew. I suppose we could have requested another magician's help, but Bostwick volunteered. He seemed to think that another magician wouldn't be a very good traveling companion, especially in some place as uninviting as the wilds of Ataxia."

"Oh?" Delilah asked, sipping her own tea.

"Maybe he thought they wouldn't want to be around goblins," Millicent said.

"What an absurd notion! Goblins and magicians get along swimmingly."

"I think he just has a pretty poor opinion of other magicians in general," Emmaline said. "I used to think that something bad might have happened to him at the Academy, and that's why he's so…"

"Bostwickian," Delilah offered.

"Sure. But after traveling with him for a year, I get the feeling he's been that way forever, and his troubles with the other students were more a matter of strong personalities grating against each other."

"But what if the students gave him a hard time about being from a famous servant family?" Millicent said. "He seems sensitive about that."

"Nonsense," Delilah said. "He should be happy to come from such an illustrious family, especially now that he gets to fulfill his destiny as a butler."

"I think that's actually what's causing most of the problems, at this point." Emmaline murmured.

"Hmm. Bostwick is quite the interesting individual, isn't he? Where is he, anyway? I want chocolate!"

"He's probably—"

"Bostwiiiiiiiiiiick!" the queen yelled into the castle over whatever Millicent was going to say.

"I'm coming!" they heard him call up the stairs. A minute later, he came into the room, panting and carrying a tray with three mugs and a plate of cookies.

"Ah, my hot cocoa!" Delilah said, taking a cup. She sipped it slowly, then, without warning spit it into Bostwick's face.

"You call this *hot* cocoa? It's tepid as a corpse! You're fired!"

"Really?" Bostwick asked hopefully, mopping his face with his sleeve.

"No, because if you were ever to leave my services before a hundred years, I would make it so everything you touched turned to cheese. Now heat this up."

Bostwick started to cast a spell, but Delilah stopped him.

"Now, Bostwick, I don't think some magic flame spell will warm the whole cup properly. No, you should go to the kitchen and heat up the whole thing over a large fire. That is what kitchens are for."

"But I'll have to go all the way down and then come back up again. It'll take forever."

"Yes, but that is a sacrifice I'm willing to make. Now off with you."

Muttering something under his breath, Bostwick left the room.

"Use oven mitts!" Delilah called after him.

"I wish you wouldn't give him such a hard time, Delilah," said Millicent. "It's mean."

Delilah looked shocked, as if it had never occurred to her that what she had been doing the past few weeks could possibly be construed as "mean".

"But, we're all having fun, right?"

"Bostwick doesn't seem to be. He's been working really hard. We're all having a party while he's running around getting us things. That can't be very nice for him."

Delilah looked thoughtful, then started purring quietly. She brought her knees up to her chest, wrapped her arms around her legs, and put her head down. After several minutes of awkward silence from Millicent and purring from Delilah, the goblin raised her head again.

"So, what you're saying is, I shouldn't make Bostwick work?"

"Well, not so much," Millicent said.

"But he tried to steal my Domino."

"That was for my sake," Emmaline interjected.

"And he didn't get away with it," Millicent said.

"So what you're both saying is, Bostwick is not as bad as he seems, so I shouldn't torture him *so* much? Well, I guess that's true. He does amuse me so. Hmm."

She continued purring, her head down once more, until Bostwick returned, carrying the tray of now steaming cocoa with an expression of great irritation on his face. He set the tray unceremoniously on the table.

"Well, it's hot now. Don't burn your tongue. And, hey, if you need another ridiculously trivial thing, don't hesitate to ask," he said, sounding unusually annoyed, even for him.

"Oh, Bostwick," Delilah said, going over to him. "I see what's going on. You feel left out and lonely. Very well, you may stay. Perhaps we shall put your lovely brown hair up in pigtails, hmm?"

"Yeah. Let's not."

"Very well then. I, in my infinite largesse, shall give you the night off."

"Why?" he asked suspiciously.

"Eh? Because I feel like it, of course."

"Yes, but what's the catch?"

"There's no catch. I'm just being nice. Plus, I honestly

can't think of anything else for you to do right now."

"But you'll think of something as soon as I've gone all the way downstairs, then call me back up, right? And I'm sure you'll do the same thing over and over again throughout the night."

"I promise I shall not call for you again until tomorrow morning. Heck, let's even say I'll wait for the sun to come up, okay?"

"For some reason, I don't believe you."

"I swear, Bostwick. I swear on my father's grave, and Millie's eyes, and on each of Emmaline's lucky rabbit's feet."

"I never really thought of them as lucky," Emmaline whispered to Millicent, who giggled.

"Fine," said Bostwick, and left.

"Of course, as soon as he falls asleep, we'll do all manner of tricks on him," Delilah said with glee.

Bostwick walked down the corridor leading to his room and noticed how quiet the castle was. The only sound he could hear was the hum of crickets out in the garden. He hadn't had an actual day off in a long time, considering that he'd been traveling with Emmaline for more than a year. When he got to his room, he sat on his bed and took out his pocket watch. After ten minutes, Delilah still hadn't called him back upstairs. Deciding that she'd keep her promise, Bostwick took from his hat a book of poems. Unbeknownst to anyone, even Emmaline, he was an avid lover of poetry, particularly that written by the acclaimed Aelfreda Ruzicka. He had become thoroughly absorbed in what he read, not noticing how much time was going by, when a dark form flitted across the open window.

"Who's there?" he asked, snapping his fingers to brighten the gas lamps around the room. Sitting on the windowsill was the cat from the counterfeit shop. "Oh, it's you. How'd you get in here?"

"The garden," he said, flicking his tail.

"All right, but what are you doing here?"

"I have a proposition for you." The cat leapt from the window to Bostwick's bed and sat, curling his tail around his feet. "Suppose you get something for me, and in exchange, I help you escape from Delilah."

"And how exactly would you do that, being a cat and all?"

"It's true, in this form I am virtually powerless, but in my goblin form, my powers rival all the goblin royalty of Ataxia. And all I need to regain those powers is the Domino of Nonpareil, which Delilah has in her possession."

"Yeah, about that… I already tried stealing it from her, which is why I'm in this predicament."

"Really? Why would you need the Domino?" the cat asked, sounding genuinely surprised.

"It's not for me. I'm helping a friend of mine. She's a rabbit."

"With my help, *both* of you could escape without getting cursed."

"Even if that's true, I can't accept your offer."

"Why not?"

"I barely know you. The Styx goblins sealed your power away for some reason. Who knows, you could have been…"

"What?"

"I don't know, some sort of monster or criminal. The point is, every time I've dealt with goblins, something bad has happened. Besides, if your plan doesn't work, Delilah will be even more angry with me. I'm already on her bad side; I wouldn't be surprised if she's got an even worse one. It all comes down to the fact that I have absolutely no reason to believe you can do what you say you can. Sorry."

"Well, perhaps I'm being too mysterious. Allow me to properly introduce myself. My name is Sebastian. I was indeed cursed to seal my power, but I swear, I would never use it against you, magician."

Bostwick noticed that when he said this, it was with an air of respect, which was odd, considering that most goblins abhorred human magic.

"Since we're doing introductions, my name's Bostwick von Dogsbody."

"And the girl who was with you at the shop?"

"Millicent. I don't know her last name."

"And is she a prisoner here too?"

"I'm pretty sure, although I don't know her offense."

"There are so many of you, it almost seems irresponsible to let you all stay captive, but still, I can't help you like this. I wish I could do something to show you that I'm trustworthy." Sebastian's ears shot up suddenly and he sat perfectly still.

Bostwick listened, but heard nothing.

"I think I'd better leave," the cat said simply, "for the time being at least."

With that, he hopped back to the window, looked briefly at the door, then leapt out into the night. Curious as to what the cat's concern had been, Bostwick opened the door and stepped out, tripped over something soft and bony, and fell right onto his face. He sat up and saw Delilah, on all fours, rubbing her back, while Emmaline and Millicent stood behind her, each holding a feather and looking guilty.

"Ouch," Delilah said. "Watch where you're going, Bostwick."

"What the… you were listening in on me!"

"What? Don't be paranoid."

"Yes, you were! Why else would you be hunched over right outside my door?"

"I was looking for a misplaced earring. They," she pointed to Millicent and Emmaline, "were helping me. Let's see, it's pink and shiny, like a… ah, there it is!" she exclaimed, picking up the earring. "You've no idea the pain that a lost earring causes, Bostwick. But you don't care about that, not you. You just like to be mean and accuse people of eavesdropping. Sniff. You're so cruel."

"Sorry," Bostwick said flatly, "but what was I supposed to think?"

"That's okay. I forgive you!" she said and without warning threw her arms around Bostwick and hugged him. It made his skin crawl. Upon being released, he stepped back several paces, almost walking into Emmaline.

"Now that that's over with," Delilah began, "I must ask, who were you talking to?"

Bostwick almost fell over a second time. "You *were* listening," he grumbled.

"Never said I wasn't. To tell the truth, we came down here to put whipped cream in your hand and then tickle your nose, but I heard a second voice behind the door and simply had to hear your conversation. Something about being trustworthy, yes?"

"I'm not telling you anything you didn't already hear. After all, I am allowed some privacy, right?"

"Friends don't keep secrets from one another." She produced a handkerchief and dabbed her eyes theatrically before tossing it away. "You could at least tell me who it was, or else I can ask the reflection in the window to show me, much the same as my mirror."

Bostwick hadn't thought of that. The queen would know everything that went on in her castle.

"Fine. It was a talking black and white cat. Happy now?"

"Wow, Bostwick. You really believed me about the windows? Gullible. Anyways, a talking cat, hmm? Why would he want to talk to you, unless," she narrowed her eyes, "he was trying to find out my innermost secrets, that only my loyal and beloved butler would know."

"He didn't ask for any secrets," Bostwick said blankly. It was technically true.

Delilah shut her eyes and shrugged.

"Ah, well, I don't really care. What would a cat want anyway? Little Mittens couldn't be scheming too much, right? Most devious plans at least require the perpetrator to have opposable thumbs…"

She trailed off and looked at Emmaline significantly.

"You couldn't possibly think a cat would've planted those bombs, Delilah."

"I wouldn't put it past a cat to do anything like that."

Bostwick sighed. "That's not what you said four

sentences ago."

"Who keeps track of such things? Don't be petty, Bostwick. Now what did you say the cat's name was?"

"I didn't say, but he calls himself Sebastian."

Delilah pouted her lips out, apparently thinking. After a moment, she clapped her hands together and cried, "Bitey McMean Monster!"

"Um…"

"That must be him. He always did claim his name was Sebastian, but I knew better. He was my little kitty when I was younger. I found him one day while strolling in the castle dungeons. So he's behind these bombing, eh? Figures."

"We don't have any concrete evidence that it's him," said Emmaline, although from what Bostwick had told her of their meeting in the shop, Sebastian's apparent grudge against Styx did make him the most likely suspect.

"Pshaw, I'm sure it's him. He's always been a wretched little beast, angry at the world, I suppose."

"I wonder why," said Bostwick sarcastically. An image of little Delilah squeezing an infuriated Sebastian flashed across his mind. "Anyway, it's supposed to be my night off, and I don't want to spend it talking about cats. Could you kindly leave?"

"Rude!" Delilah said. "I'll double, no, triple your workload tomorrow for that last remark. And you'll be getting up at the crack of dawn to do it!"

This turned out to be a wonderfully empty promise. Bostwick woke at the same time as usual to find the castle almost entirely deserted. Emmaline and Millicent didn't come down from the tower till well after noon, and even when they did they were rubbing their eyes and yawning.

"We stayed up until sunrise," Emmaline explained, as she turned back into a rabbit and let Millicent run upstairs to give the Domino back to Delilah. "We played this goblin card game, which I couldn't make heads or tails of, brushed each other's hair, drank more tea than I thought it would be possible to consume in one evening, and played truth or dare."

"Learn anything interesting?"

"Millicent has never broken a bone and is terrified of eels. Delilah has never kissed a boy and is an egomaniac. And I had to eat a handful of pickled carrots. What about you? What did that cat say to you last night?"

"He wants the Domino to change back, same as you, only he's a goblin. He said if I got it for him, he'd help us escape."

"That's way too suspicious! You can't trust him."

"I know," Bostwick said. "I'm not completely naïve."

"That's up for debate," Delilah said, whisking past them and walking away down the hall as Millicent came downstairs wearing a yellow dress and gingham apron.

"She wants us to work in the garden this afternoon. Don't worry, it'll be fun."

Bostwick picked Emmaline up and followed Millicent to yet another secret door, this time leading to a stone stairway outside that went down to the garden. They came to the entrance of a hedge maze, where a sign read, in neat, round hand writing: *Beware of Worms*. Bostwick followed Millicent in, going left and right over and over. He was thoroughly turned around by the time they came out into a small plaza, which was surprisingly civilized. Stone paths ran between plots of rose bushes and twisted locust trees, and the whole area was bordered by topiary chess pieces. Here, Delilah—dressed in a half black, half white dress with a zigzag row of hearts down the center—sat on a wicker chair.

"What do you think of my garden, Bostwick?"

"It doesn't seem very... goblin-esque."

"Goblinical is the word you're thinking of, and that's nonsense. Why, just because we are lovers of chaos doesn't mean that we can't appreciate organization. Is that paradox not goblinical on its own? But, I will admit, it's missing something. It's all so green. You don't think you could turn some of the leaves white, could you? That way, we can tell which chess pieces belong to which side."

"You mean with magic?" he said hopefully.

"How else?"

Bostwick put Emmaline down and examined one of the pawns. Changing something's color wasn't difficult, but changing all the leaves on a bush this size would be. He held his hands over the bush and willed it to turn color. It changed from dark green to snow white in an instant, though many of the leaves remained unchanged.

"It may take a while," he told the queen, hoping not to invoke her wrath.

"Take your time," she said airily. "In the meantime, Emmaline, why don't you explore the hedge maze? It goes all over, you know."

Happy to be outside of the castle for a change, Emmaline obeyed, hopping back into the maze. She thought it best to try and retrace Millicent's steps from a moment ago to find her way out again. However, try as she might, she couldn't find an exit. Realizing after some time that she was completely lost, she wondered if perhaps there was some trick to it. She tried counting turns and going backward, but everything looked the same, especially from such a low angle. At last, she saw something sky blue through the leaves of the hedge in front of her. She hopped forward to see what it was, but was in no way reassured by what she found.

Bostwick had finally finished turning the pawns white and was about to move on to the rooks when something caught his eye. Several hedgerows away, standing ten feet tall, was a blue, scaly beast. It had two bat-like wings folded against its back, and a long neck leading to its horned head. From this distance, it was difficult to tell, but it looked like the nostrils at the end of its long snout were smoking.

"What on earth is that?" Bostwick said, crouching behind the topiary to keep out of the beast's sight.

"A worm," Delilah replied, taking a sip of iced tea.

"Worm?"

"W-Y-R-M. Wyrm."

"Oh!" said Millicent, who had written the sign.

"'Wyrm' as in 'dragon'?" Bostwick asked.

"Oh, Bostwick!" said the queen. "Dragons are a completely different species. Much bigger, and with four legs instead of just the two."

"I am not working in a garden with that thing!"

"Calm down, Bostwick. Wyrms are a dime a dozen in

Ataxia. A common garden pest, really."

"I've never seen one ever, anywhere."

"Well, you obviously weren't looking properly. Anyway, they're as gentle as can be if you don't provoke them."

Bostwick hesitantly went back to work, but froze mid-spell.

"What do wyrms eat?"

"Oh, the usual: gophers, rats, rabbits. They'd be quite useful for keeping vermin away, if they didn't have a habit of breathing fire."

Before she could say more, Bostwick dashed into the hedge.

"How rude. He hasn't even finished with the rooks. What do you suppose has gotten into him?"

Delilah and Millicent looked at each other. "Emmaline," they said together, and raced after the magician.

Bostwick was trying to find a way around the maze when he heard Delilah say behind him, "Move." The hedges parted before him, revealing the wyrm in its entirety. It was staring down at the ground, where a frightened Emmaline stood stock-still.

"Emmaline, run!" Bostwick said.

The wyrm plunged its head towards the ground. Emmaline hopped backwards, just in time to avoid being eaten, but one of her legs got badly scratched as she pulled it past one of the wyrm's sharp teeth. The wyrm only looked slightly put out, but glanced at Bostwick and swung its long tail across the magician's chest, sending him to the ground. It didn't want him to scare away its prey. Emmaline was about to hop into the hedge behind her, but the beast sent a stream of fire from its mouth, setting the foliage ablaze. She had nowhere to run, and the fire was too large for Bostwick to put out with magic.

Bostwick jumped to his feet, grabbed a branch lying on the ground nearby and turned it into a bird, which he threw towards the wyrm in an effort to distract it. The wyrm snapped up the bird in one bite, then turned back to Emmaline. Next, Bostwick conjured the mallet he used for destroying pocket watches and hit down on the reptilian tail. That got its attention. The beast turned an angry gaze on Bostwick, and charged towards him so fast that he had to jump into the hedge behind him to avoid being trampled. The wyrm now stood in the center of the topiary plaza. It shot angry flames around it indiscriminately, scorching three pawns and part of the white knight, and finally made a loud screeching noise.

"Good going, Bostwick, now you made it mad," Delilah said. "And look, he brought a friend."

A larger wyrm, awakened by the commotion, flew down to the clearing where the first one had stood. It looked from Bostwick to the rabbit, as if wondering if it could finish the job its companion couldn't. Bostwick was in no position to help Emmaline, having become tangled in branches in his haste to get out of the other beast's way. Sure that she was done for, he shut his eyes, unable to watch the inevitable event.

"Stop!" Millicent cried.

Bostwick opened his eyes just in time to see Millicent holding a deck of cards, shooting card after card at the wyrm's eyes. Bostwick was in awe. Millicent was doing magic.

Since when could she do magic?

The wyrm shook its head, annoyed, and swung its tail toward Millicent. She rolled under it, and, keeping low to the ground, took the opportunity to run over and snatch up Emmaline. The other wyrm had by now come back towards its companion, walking past Bostwick and Delilah like they weren't even there.

Surrounded by wyrms on one side and fire on the other, Millicent didn't have many options. She shut her eyes tight, thrust her arm out toward the flames, and screamed "Disappear!"

At first it seemed like nothing had happened, then the hedge vanished from sight, as did the flames engulfing it, and Millicent ran back into the maze. The wyrm who had first appeared looked at the second as if questioning if they should even bother running after her. The second one replied by shooting a series of fireballs out over the maze, catching a large portion of plants on fire. Apparently, wyrms were sore losers.

Delilah floated into the air, hovering over the maze to see where Millicent had gone. One of the wyrms shot a stream of flame at her, which caught the hem of her dress on fire.

"That does it!" she said furiously, and landed. "Bostwick, start putting out this fire. I'm going to deal with these stupid beasts."

"It's too big to put out all at once."

"Can't you conjure water?" she asked, approaching the wyrms, which he could have sworn were laughing.

"Not enough."

"Ugh. Useless. I suppose it's up to me, then."

Unable to do anything about the fire, Bostwick instead ran into the maze to find Millicent and Emmaline. He called out to them, but only heard Delilah's voice rising over the flames.

"This," she yelled, and he heard a strange crackling sound, almost like electricity, "was one of my favorite dresses!"

He hurried along, looking for any sign of his companions, and wished he could command the plants to move as Delilah had. Finally, he found the girls—staring at yet another wyrm. Thankfully, this one was not in an attack position, but was curled, cat-like and sleeping, unaware of the fire burning around it. Unfortunately, it blocked their way and climbing over it would risk waking it up.

"Should we go back?" Emmaline asked, coughing.

"I don't know the way," Millicent said. "The maze changed when Delilah told it to move."

She sounded congested, and Bostwick noticed, too, that it was getting harder to breath. Suddenly, from the base of one of the hedges jumped a small black and white form. It was Sebastian.

"Follow me," he said. The cat scurried onward, only looking back every so often to make sure the humans were keeping up. They seemed to be going in circles, the flames spreading around them all the while. They came across a hog-sized wyrm, most likely a baby, that opened its mouth to breath fire at them as soon as it saw them, but the cat swiped it across the nose with his paw and sent it slinking away. Finally, they came out onto the path leading to the front door of the castle. They were all relieved to have fresh air, but

Millicent looked back toward the maze.

"Where's Delilah?"

Her question was answered as the queen came out from another entrance, followed by the small wyrm who was trotting after her like a puppy.

"Ah, so you're all safe," she said, patting the wyrm on the head. "But did you really have to pick on Brutus here? He's just a hatchling."

"He was trying to attack us," Sebastian said.

Delilah's eyes lighted on him and her face became stony.

"So you finally decided to show up?"

The cat was about to reply, but there was a crash from within the hedge.

"Delilah," said Millicent, "what about the fire?"

"The wyrms have been disciplined; they're putting it out."

"But…"

"They'll be all right. Really, they were just mad that you hit them, Bostwick. It was uncalled for."

"They were going to eat me!" Emmaline said.

"I'm sure if you explained that you weren't really a rabbit, they would've understood."

"So what, they can talk now?" Bostwick asked, patting away a cinder that he'd noticed on his shoulder.

"Don't be silly," she said, looking the baby wyrm in the eye. "You can't talk at all, can you?"

The wyrm sneezed in reply, which sent Delilah into a fit of laughter.

"You shouldn't be so casual with people's lives," said Sebastian.

"You all take everything much too seriously. Everyone's

alive, aren't they?"

"Yes, no thanks to you. From what I saw, Bostwick and the maid did most of the work, though I think," said the cat, looking at Millicent, "you were attempting to make the flames vanish instead of the hedge itself."

All eyes were on Millicent. In trying to escape from the fire, they had forgotten her magical exploits. She turned bright red.

"I, um, I would've told you, but, um…"

"Inside!" Delilah commanded. "We'll discuss everything inside. After all, the wyrms won't want to be distracted by our standing around. They really do have the most sensitive egos, you know?"

Six

Incantations, Explanations, Complications, and Charms

Delilah spent considerable time supervising the wyrms' fire retardation. Meanwhile, everyone, including Sebastian, gathered in the upstairs library, with orders not to talk until the queen got back. Bostwick sat at one of the tables, healing Emmaline's scratches inside of a shoebox. Sebastian wandered from shelf to shelf, looking over book titles. Millicent sat by herself in an armchair, with her hands folded and her head down, looking miserable. No one spoke.

They had begun to wonder what was taking Delilah so long when she showed up pushing a food cart laden with pineapple chunks, pineapple upside-down cake, and a ham and pineapple casserole, as well as a pitcher filled with pineapple juice. Everything appeared to be fairly well made, if unimaginative.

"Now," Delilah said, after handing plates of food to everyone, although no one was particularly hungry, "I believe some explanations are in order, starting with you, Paddy-Paws McFlicky Tail."

"My name is Sebastian," he said, flattening his ears to his head.

"It doesn't matter what you're called. I want to know why you're here in Styx, particularly in my garden."

"Maybe I'm just trying to relive old times. We had such fun together, didn't we?" His tail twitched wildly in irritation.

"Why were you talking to my butler, then? Conspiring about something?"

"We were discussing his rabbit companion, since she and I have the same... condition. I was asking him if he'd found any sort of cure for it, as I have obviously yet to do so."

"So it seems," Delilah said, taking a sip of juice. "So, you had no luck after running away, hmm? Where did you go, anyway?"

"I visited several places. Mostly, I lived in the Wastes."

From what Emmaline and Bostwick could tell, this could not have been pleasant. When they first came to Ataxia, they had passed through the Wastes, a barren land to the west of Styx Castle, though part of the country itself. All they had seen there were dark-fruited trees, jagged black stones, miles of red earth, and, scattered here and there, enormous piles of rubbish. It seemed to be an uninhabited place where Styxians discarded their garbage, not the sort of place any normal person would call home.

"Hmm," Delilah continued, "and did you learn any new tricks there? How to make explosives, perhaps?"

"No," Sebastian said, sounding even more annoyed. His tail lashed faster.

"Come clean! You're the mad bomber! You're trying to destroy Styx! We know all about it."

"I've no idea about bombs and I do not want to destroy anyone."

"Don't play dumb. You hate Styx, always have, you spiteful little cretin."

"Delilah!" It was Millicent, speaking for the first time. "Please, I'm sure he's not the one behind those bombings. He saved our lives. He wouldn't have done that if he was just going to kill us anyway." She turned to the cat. "Thank you, by the way."

"Not at all," the cat replied, bowing his head. "But if I may, why didn't you just vanish the other hedges around you to clear a path through the maze?"

Millicent seemed to shrink where she sat.

"I wasn't really thinking when I did it the first time. I was only trying to vanish the flames, anyway."

"I didn't know you could do magic at all," Emmaline said, hopping down from the table and over to Millicent's chair.

"Why didn't you tell us?" Bostwick asked.

Delilah got a slightly livid expression behind her mask, and Bostwick immediately regretted his question.

"Well, I suppose I was embarrassed," Millicent began. "I'm horrible at magic, and you were at the top of your class and everything. I mean, I didn't want someone who had graduated from the Academy to see my magic when I, well... I guess now that you know, I should tell the whole story..."

When Millicent was six years old, she saw her first magic show. A traveling magician came to South Wellington, where she, her three sisters, and their parents lived. The magician was mediocre, and most of the people of the town had seen better, but to the young Millicent, he was the most clever and amazing man she'd ever seen, and there was nothing, ever, in the entire world, that could be better than doing magic. After the show, he invited the crowd forward to ask questions. Few people stayed until the end, so lousy was his act, and even fewer came to question him, knowing his answer would be that all ticket sales were final. When Millicent got her turn to speak to him, she did not mince words.

"How do you do magic?" she asked.

"It takes years of practice, at only the finest institution," he said, producing a brochure for Melieh's Academy of Magic from thin air and handing it to her, "and, of course, you have to have 'The Gift'."

She looked at him questioningly, so he went on.

"You have to be able to do magic. Any. Even a little. Of course, for most people, that is impossible."

"How do you know if you can do it?"

The magician straightened up, thinking.

"Well, you just sort of… You have to will something to happen, but you have to will it the right way, and usually there are some props or hand gestures. It's hard to explain."

This feeble explanation was enough for the young girl, who raced home to prove the magic ability she was sure she had. She thought that a good trick to try would be making something vanish, because it seemed so much easier than making something appear. She decided to use one of the rocks in her mother's garden because no one was fond of this particular rock—at least she wasn't, and that if she couldn't make it reappear, it wouldn't be missed. She cupped the rock in her hands, closed her eyes and willed, in what she assumed was the right way, for the rock to vanish. She opened her eyes to find the rock unchanged. She tried shaking it and turning it over, but to no effect. After several more failed attempts, she dropped the rock and swung back towards town to question the magician further.

Something green whipped past her and she froze, but saw nothing. She looked left, and saw another flash of green, and there, clinging to her shoulder, was a strand of light, leaf green hair. She ran inside to get a better look in the mirror. Sure enough, all of the hair on her head, her eyebrows, and even her lashes had turned green. She smiled, because she knew it was magic. Unintentional, but still magic. Her joy was cut short by a shriek from her mother, who ran in, grabbed at Millicent's hair, and asked what on earth had happened. Millicent explained about the magician and the stone, sure it would calm her mother's worries.

It did not.

"Green hair, by accident? Good gracious! What if you turned your skin green? What if you caught the house on fire? You will absolutely not do any more magic!"

Millicent burst into tears, for her life's dream, only that day realized, was now over. Once her mother got her quieted down and was herself more clear headed, she made a compromise.

"It's obvious you can do magic, and it might not be a bad undertaking, in the long run, but it's too dangerous to practice on your own. Now, you can go to the library and get books on magic, and learn what you can that way, but you're not to *do* magic unless you get admitted to that academy.

Now let's go find that magician so he can fix your hair."

But the magician was nowhere to be seen, having already left for the next town. Millicent's mother was furious, but Millicent said she didn't mind, because green was close to yellow, and yellow was her favorite color.

When Millicent went to the library to find magic books, she was sorely disappointed to find that they didn't even have a special section for magic, and shelved the books they did have under *Theatre*. Even more disappointing was that the books themselves were merely three ancient volumes of handwritten notes that were coming apart at the seams. The only reason they were even in that good of condition, the librarian said, was because they had never been checked out.

Undaunted, Millicent set to work learning everything she could from the three books. This proved difficult, not because the handwriting was poor or the ink smudged, but because the author had an extremely circuitous way of addressing any one topic. The first volume was littered with diagrams, incantations, and descriptions of spells, followed by philosophical explanations that went on so long that they occasionally became rants, and only after pages and pages of this did actual instructions for how to perform the spell appear. The second volume was much the same, though the philosophical sections were cut down to succinct paragraphs, and they were absent from the third volume entirely.

Most of the spells, Millicent was pleased to find, had very practical applications, which pleased her more than the showy stage magic that had delighted her when she was younger. As the years went by, she memorized every word of the three volumes, which the library had graciously given her. She now knew spells to clean glass without leaving streak marks, how to float things down off of very high shelves, and how to button up any number of buttons with the snap of her fingers. She also knew much more of the theory behind magic, as well as some spells she couldn't imagine any practical use for at all, like how to cause liquids to flow backwards or how to make shadows disappear.

Now, all she wanted was to put her knowledge to use. Her thirteenth birthday was fast approaching, and thirteen was the minimum age for acceptance into the Academy. Her parents had already planned a trip to the Capital, where she would take the test to see if she could officially learn magic under the school's tutelage. She had packed a month in advance, and reread all three volumes every day, just to make sure the knowledge was fresh in her head.

When their train came into the Capital station her parents gaped at the finery of the city, but Millicent was saving her enthusiasm for when she would finally see the Academy. The next day, her father walked with her to the school gates. Millicent assured him she would be fine the rest of the way and that he could spend the hours sight-seeing instead of waiting for her. In truth, she was excited and nervous, but went in alone. In the courtyard, she met a short woman in a black dress with a slit down one side showing a red skirt underneath.

"Ah, you must be Millicent Minikin. I am Sarah Miyako, Officer of Admissions and Graduations. The test is right this way. If you have any questions, feel free to ask."

They entered the school and came into a long, wood-paneled hallway lined with square, green paper lanterns. Millicent assumed that they were magically lit, because they didn't flicker and made the hallway seem as bright as day. She saw many groups of students walking in the hall past them, the boys in black tunics with colored trim and black pants, the girls in dresses similar to Miss Miyako's, but with different colored underskirts.

"Do the different colors of uniform mean anything?" Millicent asked.

"Colors signify what level of magical proficiency you're at. From the bottom, they go yellow, green, blue, and purple, though once you master everything and graduate, if you're a girl, you can wear any color, though red is traditional. Boys usually wear tailcoats and cummerbunds of whatever color during performances."

They continued on, and Millicent was impressed by the number of purple-clad students. She would be happy just to wear yellow, though she didn't say this aloud. They came to a spiraling staircase and climbed for four stories. Millicent was out of breath when they reached the top, but Miyako continued at a swift pace to a door at the end of the hall. Behind this was a small, cramped-feeling room with a desk in the center, which was facing a long table with three sets of paper and pens. At this table sat two men, both wearing tailcoats with red cummerbunds. Miyako gestured for Millicent to sit in the desk, while she herself took the remaining chair behind the table.

"Now, we're going to test how much raw magic ability you have, and how much control you have over it."

With a wave of her hand, Miyako conjured a vase of three roses onto Millicent's desk.

"Now, you're going to attempt to perform some basic tricks. It doesn't matter if you do them well or not; just do what you can. Please take one of the roses."

Millicent did as she was told, taking out the rose with shaking fingers. For the first time, doubt entered her mind. What if she couldn't do it? After all, she'd only performed one spell, at an extremely young age, and even that had been somewhat accidental. She stared at the rose, all her confidence sapped, and waited for the next instruction.

"First, please cause the flower to float."

Millicent breathed a sigh of relief. She'd read about this. It was simple, really. All she had to do was will the flower to rise, while trying, magically, to negate the pull the earth had on it. Of course, the book had never really said how to do that, but it was a start at least. Millicent held her hand perfectly flat, balancing the stem on her palm. She tried, with all her might, to make it rise. She waited while nothing happened, then began to count the seconds. Her hand started to shake as terror crept its way into her mind, and then, about to give up, she closed her eyes and gasped. She dropped the rose to the floor, for it had caught on fire. Miyako stood up and waved her hand, vanishing the burning flower. The two men to her right scribbled something down on their papers while Miyako wrote one word in a single sweeping motion.

Millicent was sure she would be told to leave, but Miyako simply asked if she was all right and would like to continue. Millicent nodded, though the answer was negative to both questions.

"Next, please turn one of the flowers into a handkerchief. It can be of any color."

Millicent pulled the next flower out. She decided that whatever happened, it couldn't be worse than starting a fire. Thinking wildly, she waved the rose around in what she thought was a magical way, ending in a determined flick. To her supreme surprise, the petals spun and popped, each turning into a miniature red handkerchief. The men wrote more cryptic notes.

"Well done," Miyako said, smiling. "Now, for the last test, please vanish the final rose."

Her ego somewhat bolstered by her semi-success, Millicent took the final rose and concentrated. She hoped with all her might that the flower would vanish, or wilt, or at least that her hair wouldn't change color again. Instead, one of the fountain pens on the long table exploded, sending ink everywhere, including that magician's white shirt.

"I'm sorry!" Millicent cried.

"Quite all right," the man replied, dabbing the ink from the paper in front of him rather than from his clothes. Miyako stood up and took the rose from Millicent, who'd forgotten that she was holding anything, and gestured for her to follow.

"Well, that wasn't too bad, now was it?" Miyako asked when they were out in the hall again.

"It was horrible. I could barely do one trick."

"Well, you're just starting out, after all. No one does well on their first try. Why do you think we have three separate roses? I've seen much worse than that, believe me. Now for the written test."

"Written?" Millicent asked, panicking. She hadn't heard about any writing. What if they tested her about spells she didn't know?

"It's nothing to worry about. It's more of a personality test, really. Just to see what sort of magician you might turn out to be. I've never heard of anyone failing it."

She led the way to another room, this one much larger and airier than the first, with a large window looking out on the courtyard. There was again a desk in the center, but instead of a table, an armchair sat at the front of the room facing out towards the window.

"If you need anything, just ask," Miyako said, sitting in the armchair.

Millicent took her own seat and examined the test, which consisted of a series of open-ended hypothetical and philosophical questions on several sheets of paper. As she looked over the questions, she was filled with relief. Many of them dealt with topics she'd studied in the handwritten volumes back home. Some of the questions were a little more difficult, asking about principles of magic, such as its purpose, power, and limitations, but Millicent answered to the best of her knowledge, based on information from the volumes and her own somewhat naïve philosophy about the world. She was finished in what felt like no time, although when she stood to tell Miyako, she found her to be fast asleep.

"Sorry, it's these spring afternoons, always getting to me," she said, once Millicent had summoned enough courage to wake her.

Miyako led her back down to the street, and waited with her for her father to arrive.

"So, how long will it take for them to decide?" Millicent asked.

"You should know within two days. We'll send a letter to your hotel with details. Don't worry; I think you have a lot of promise."

Two days came and went, but it was not until the third day that a letter arrived; it said simply to come back to the Academy. Millicent didn't know whether this was good or bad, but she assumed that the lack of information signaled something amiss. Perhaps they had lost her written test, or couldn't read through the black stains on the notes of the magician she'd splattered with ink. Her suspicions were confirmed by the grim expression Miyako wore when she returned to the Academy the next day. Miyako led the way inside again, but said nothing. They again climbed the staircase, but this time went to the sixth and top floor.

"Um, Miss Miyako…" Millicent began nervously.

"The president wants to speak with you personally," she said simply.

They came to a large double door. Millicent waited while Miyako went inside to announce her arrival. She came back out within seconds, and beckoned Millicent inside. The president's office was a large room lined with polished, cherry wood paneled walls, bookshelves, and several chairs. At the far end of the room was a large desk, behind which was a window looking out on the street. An elderly man in the finest magician regalia sat at the desk, but stood when Millicent approached.

"Miss Millicent Minikin," he said, "I am Eustis Wilfrock, president of Melieh's."

It was a standard introduction, but after this, he faltered, as if not knowing where to go next.

"Ah, please have a seat," he said at last, gesturing to one of the chairs. "Now, we've reviewed your admissions test, and there is, well, a problem."

Miyako seemed to bristle at this, but said nothing.

"Was it the fire?" Millicent asked miserably, "or, well, if it was the ink exploding…"

"Actually, your practical test was fine. Nothing to write home about, but no worse than most," the president said without malice, but still too-matter-of-factly to be polite. "The problem was with your written test, actually."

Miyako could contain herself no longer, and threw her arms up with theatrical flare.

"There is no problem! Honestly, can't you see the girl is as timid as a mouse? She's thirteen, for Pete's sake!"

"Well, you know what they say, 'it's always the quiet ones'."

"The test is obviously flawed."

"It was written by experts."

Miyako turned in a snarl, something Millicent would've thought such a proper women incapable of, and began to pace back and forth.

"I'm the Officer of Admissions; I should have the final say in this, not some test. I know she'll be a good magician. I can just… tell!"

"Well, if magic was based on feelings and intuition, that would be fine, but it isn't, and we have rules to abide by."

Miyako gave a low growl, much like an angry cat, and threw herself into another chair.

"At least explain the situation to her," she hissed.

The president turned to Millicent, who was now thoroughly confused.

"You see, Miss Minikin, the personality test was first administered, centuries ago, to ensure that no people of, well, ill-repute would learn magic and use it to do, shall we say, untoward deeds. Apparently, some time ago, there was a sort of rogue group of students at the Academy who were using magic for who-knows-what. The school regents of the time felt they had to administer the test to all current and, now, potential students to ensure the same thing would not happen again. The test examines a student's attitudes about magic, as well as the world in general. Most students pass, but if a student fails, that is, if they show evidence of megalomania, psychopathy, or other criminal lunacies, then they are denied entrance to the Academy."

Here he paused and fiddled with the chain of his pocket watch, apparently to stall for time. With a sigh, he looked her straight in the eye, then looked at his left shoulder.

"You failed."

As what he had just said added up in Millicent's head, she felt everything sinking. She sat and thought, while Miyako fumed and the president looked around his office, as if searching for a way to escape from telling a young girl that she was malignantly insane. At last, Millicent spoke.

"Am I… a bad person?"

"No, dear," Miyako said hastily.

"Well," the president began, "probably not, but the test

seems to think so. And the rules are absolute; we can't allow you to study here."

Millicent finally understood what people meant when they said they were heart broken. She physically displayed the empty feeling in her chest by crying. Even if it was in front of the most powerful magician in the entire Empire, she couldn't help it.

"The Academy has never denied admission to anyone who can do magic!" Miyako growled.

"No one's ever failed the test before, as far as I know."

Millicent sobbed, unable to stop herself, and both magicians looked at her. Miyako only became angrier at the injustice of it all; who ever heard of an evil overlord crying like a little girl? The president, on the other hand, was at a loss. On the one hand, the rule stood, and the president of long ago had obviously known what he was doing. On the other, he himself, Eustis Wilfrock, was the father of six girls, and the sight of tears proved almost too much for him. This girl was obviously not a threat to anyone currently, but her test had been such a puzzlement. Most of the answers perfectly fit what the administrators had considered a criminal mind, but every so often, there were answers concerning the girl's love of daffodils and her intense dislike for seeing any living creature in pain. It was true what Miyako had said: the girl seemed to be a lovely person, but as the head of the Academy, he had the rest of the students' welfare to think of, and there still existed the possibility that this girl might turn out, after all, to be a nasty character. If only there was some way to let her learn what she could, without endangering any of the other students.

"Wait a moment," he said happily. "I think I might have the solution."

"She can stay?"

"Well, no, but there is a sort of loophole we can employ. Miyako, fetch me von Dogsbody!"

"You want him to teach her? He's just a student."

"Don't be ridiculous! He's good, but not that good, yet. No, we need stationery, pronto."

"Yes, sir!" Miyako said and stood to leave.

"Ah, and Miyako, make sure it's colorful, and shiny, if possible."

"Uh, yes, sir," she said, and hurried out of the room.

"Now, I've no idea if this will work or not, but we'll try. Now, Miss Minikin," he said, conjuring a handkerchief and handing it to her, "I suggest you go back to your hotel and rest a bit."

"All right," she said, dabbing her eyes.

"And don't worry, Miss Minikin. I think, if everything works out, you'll become a fine magician. When your father wrote to us, he said you did your first spell when you were only six."

"My hair," she said, sniffling, "but it was sort of an accident. I was trying to make a rock disappear and failed."

"Now, now, just because things don't turn out exactly as you expected doesn't make it a failure. Magic at six years of age is nothing to sneeze at."

"Really?" she asked, brightening for the first time all day.

"Indeed."

Millicent smiled proudly, and after returning to him a somewhat damp handkerchief, left his office, assuring him that she could find the way out on her own.

The president smiled to himself, but hoped he was doing the right thing. He felt that everything would be fine, but, as he had said, magic wasn't based on feelings and intuition.

Millicent remembered the entire event, but only told choice parts to her companions: her hair turning green, studying the spells in the three magic volumes, taking the tests and, in conclusion, the simple fact that she had failed. That day had been, perhaps, her worst ever, and she did not want to relive it out loud.

"But, wait," Bostwick said when Millicent finished, "that makes no sense."

Everyone looked at him. What he said was true, but so obvious it needed no response.

"First of all," he continued, "that test is impossible to fail. It's just impossible."

"I know," Millicent said, thoroughly embarrassed.

"But *you*? I mean, even if someone were to fail it, it wouldn't be you. That test is supposed to ferret out evil geniuses and dark overlord types. You wouldn't hurt a fly."

"It's true," Delilah added. "I asked her to catch some for my pet frog once, and she just didn't have the heart to do it."

"Then why?" Bostwick asked, still baffled by the entire situation.

"Clearly the test is flawed," Delilah said, "or else Millie has been deceiving us all, and is actually plotting our doom as we speak."

Millicent chuckled a bit at this, but still looked gloomy.

"So you see," she said, "I didn't want to tell you I could use magic because, really, I'm no good at it."

"That's just because you haven't had much practice," Bostwick said sympathetically. "No one's good when they first start out."

"I bet you were," she said miserably.

It was somewhat true, but Bostwick didn't want to admit it at a time like this.

"Well, Millicent," Emmaline said, sitting up on her hind legs, "maybe I could put in a good word for you at the Academy. Our tea inspector holds some sway there; he's distantly related to one of the old presidents. And I'm sure they'd listen to Bostwick if he talked to them."

Millicent smiled, but hung her head.

"It doesn't work that way," she said. "But really, I'm all right. You wouldn't think it, but being a maid is actually sort of fun. I can't compare it to studying magic at the Academy, but—"

Just then, the clock struck nine. Millicent sighed.

"Well, it's getting late, so…"

"Indeed," Delilah said, "and if we don't go to bed soon, terrible monsters will enter our dreams. It's true, you know? Ah, but what to do with you," she said, addressing Sebastian.

He was not looking at her, but was focused on Millicent, though his eyes had a glazed, faraway look.

"Hey, Kitty Meow-Meow, where are you sleeping?"

He blinked and looked at her, and his air of annoyance instantly returned.

"I'll find my way around. I did live here for some time, you know."

"Just don't go skulking around the dungeons, because that's where the wyrms sleep."

"As if I would ever go back there," he said, and marched, as much as a cat can march, out of the room.

"Well, good night, everyone. Remember to turn down the lights when you leave."

And with that, the queen left.

"Well," Emmaline said at last, and hopped to the door, "I suppose we should get to bed too. Come on, Bostwick."

"In a minute."

He wanted to say something, but could not put his thoughts into words. Magic: it was the one thing other than this miserable servitude that he and Millicent shared, and had it not been for the bizarre results of the test, Millicent would have been learning at the Academy. She might not even be in Styx now, for all he knew. It was, truly, a horrible turn of events, worse even than being unable to pull a rabbit from a hat. He wanted to say some words of solidarity, something to the effect that they, as magicians, should stick together and not give up, whatever the circumstances. But Bostwick had never been eloquent, and said nothing of the sort.

"You should still try to practice magic. There are no houses to catch on fire here."

"I know," she said, smiling sheepishly, "but now I'm more afraid of making a fool of myself before a master magician. I wouldn't want to turn your hair green by accident."

"Actually, that's easy to fix. I can turn yours back right now if you want."

"No, thanks," she replied, standing up. "I'm actually a bit

proud of my hair. It was the first trick I ever performed, after all, so it's special."

"That's true, I suppose."

"So what was your first trick, anyway?"

"What?" he asked, freezing on the way to the door.

"Your first-ever magic trick. Did you do it on your own, or wait till you got to the Academy? That would probably have been a better idea, now that I think about it."

But Bostwick was silently wracking his brain for the answer. His first trick, the first time he had used magic to exert his will over something, just by thinking... when had that been? Soon, he was forced to answer truthfully and, in his mind, terribly.

"I can't remember."

"Oh... well, I guess that makes sense. You've learned so many spells, it must be hard to remember all of them, especially when it's late. We really should be going to bed."

Bostwick agreed, and they went their separate ways, though Bostwick went to Emmaline's room instead of his own. Thankfully, she was not yet asleep.

"What's the matter, Bostwick?"

"I can't remember my first spell."

"So?"

"It's important." He sat down next to Emmaline's bed, which was slightly bigger than rabbit-sized but still far too small to sit on. "It's as if I can't even remember why I became a magician. Somewhere along the way, I've become so concerned with being the best that I've lost sight of what's really important."

"And that is?"

"Magic. Just magic, in and of itself. Not being a court magician, or anything like that."

"I like you as a court magician. I don't think being a little ambitious makes you any less of a good magician."

"You don't understand," Bostwick said, absentmindedly picking up the wishing stone from Emmaline's dresser and turning it over and over in his hands.

"I suppose I don't. What's got you so worked up about this, anyway?" Then, Emmaline had to laugh. "Don't tell me Millicent's being a magician has gotten you worried."

"She's ten times the magician I am," he said sullenly. "Sure, she doesn't know much, but she loves magic and tried to understand as much as she could about it. She tried to give it her all. And yet she thinks she's some sort of failure compared to me. It's... depressing."

"Um..."

"You don't get it."

"No, Bostwick, not being magically inclined at all, I don't. But, as your friend, I have to say I believe you're a good magician, really. You're just over-thinking things."

"I wish Clarence was here," Bostwick said, unconsoled. "He'd know what to do."

Now, the wishing stone that Bostwick held, unbeknownst to him, had started that very moment to go to work. Had it been a proper wishing stone, it would have teleported Clarence there on the spot. As it was only a replica, its magic was much weaker and did not have the power to grant wishes, but instead set events in motion to bring about the desired result. As Bostwick continued to bemoan the situation, and Emmaline, fed up, chased him from her room so she could get some sleep, half-way around the world at an inn in Rockford, the idea of visiting Styx was worming its way into Clarence's dreams, only to come to fruition days later.

Seven

Concerning Clarence

"Look at that castle, Jill. Now that's art right there," Clarence said, brushing blonde hair out of his face. He stroked Jill, his pet jackalope, and walked up the cobbled path to the giant wooden door. "'Knock to ring the bell!' How marvelously whimsical!"

He rapped his knuckles in a musical pattern on the door and heard a bell ring from within the recesses of the castle. A few moments passed, which he filled by whistling a cheery tune. When the door opened, he was greeted by a girl with green hair in a maid uniform. Before she could speak, he bent down on one knee, swept up her hand in his and kissed it. The maid gasped, but Clarence, used to this reaction, went on with his introduction.

"My dear lady, allow me to introduce myself. My name is Clarence, Clarence Bellemont, and I," he said, pausing for dramatic effect, "am a door-to-door magician."

"Oh dear," the maid said, "I was afraid of that."

"Do not be alarmed. I assure you my magic is harmless. I wish only to entertain the masses with my prestidigitation and legerdemain. I ask for but a moment of your time."

"I'm very sorry, but we don't need any magic right now," the girl responded, apparently trying to get rid of him in a hurry.

"Nonsense! Everyone needs a little magic every now and then."

"What I meant was, we already have a magician."

"Do you?" he said, brightening, if it was possible, even more. "Anyone I might know?"

For the first time, the maid was silent. She hastily looked Clarence over. Her eyes settled on Jill, and a look of comprehension came over her face.

"No," she said, shutting the door in Clarence's face. From behind the wood, he heard her say, "I'm sorry to be so rude, but it's better if you leave."

"Say no more, dear lady. I understand entirely."

This was not the case, however, because rather than leave the castle, he set to work on a plan to get himself inside. From his sleeve he pulled a long rope of colorful handkerchiefs, made the end into a lasso, and spun it round his head several times before throwing it high onto the second story of the castle. The loop caught a stone statue of a chess piece. Clarence gave the rope an experimental tug, then began to climb it without a second thought. He hauled himself and his jackalope up to the second story ledge, inched his way to an open window, and climbed in to find himself in greenhouse filled with strange overhanging foliage and speckled and striped leaves. He quickly exited through a door, which led to a hall filled with portraits of goblin royalty. A huge grin spread across his face at the thought of walking the same hallways as so many adventurous and spirited souls. He kept going until he stood before a large double door.

"This looks promising," he said to himself.

He opened one of the doors and stuck his head into what he discovered was the throne room. At the end of the room, at the foot of the throne, sat a pink haired goblin who was absorbed in a game of solitaire.

"Hello, Bostwick," she said, without looking up. "Aren't you supposed to be polishing the capybaras or something?"

"I'm afraid I'm not Bostwick," Clarence said.

The goblin glanced up for a moment, but went back to her card game, unperturbed.

"No, you definitely are not."

"This Bostwick wouldn't happen to be Bostwick von Dogsbody, would he?"

"Is he really that infamous?"

"Not nearly as infamous as yourself, Delilah of Styx."

This caught the goblin's attention. She laid down her hand of cards and stood up to properly look at Clarence.

"You're a magician, aren't you?"

"I am," he said, bowing.

"Where's your hat?"

He pulled a battered and beaten top hat out from under his coat. The top was hanging off by a few threads. He stuck his arm through it to thoroughly demonstrate its shabbiness.

Delilah laughed and smiled warmly at him.

"Now that's how a magician is meant to be. Come, my chum, how is it you know Bostwick? We shall talk over cards."

They sat down and Delilah gathered her cards together, only to deal them back out again.

♠ ♦ ♣ ♥ ♣ ♦ ♠

"Bostwiiiiiiiick!" Delilah called out the window

"I wish she wouldn't do that," Bostwick said, throwing down an enormous pair of hedge clippers. He had just finished trimming the burnt twigs off the topiary of the White Knight.

When he arrived in the throne room minutes later, he saw, to his surprise, a tall blond boy smiling at him.

"Cl-Clarence?" Bostwick said, dumbfounded.

"Surprised to see me?"

"Of course. What are you doing here? Why aren't you at the Academy?"

"I graduated this past winter. Now I'm a fully fledged door-to-door magician! And I was traveling, door-to-door as I do, when it struck me. If I wanted to see the world, I'd need to see the *whole* world, including Ataxia and Pandemonium. And wouldn't goblins like to see a little magic?"

"They can *do* magic, Clarence."

"Yes, but human-type magic must be very rare here indeed. So, I decided to come to Styx first because, well, it was closest, and also—"

"Wait. If you're serious about this, I have to warn you, goblins really don't like humans, especially magicians. They seem insulted by the fact that we can do magic at all."

"Well, of course," said Clarence, "but that adversity is what makes it an adventure. I must admit I envy you, Bostwick. Helping a princess, traveling all over Ataxia, and now serving the Queen of Styx. It's amazing."

"How did you know about all that?"

"Delilah told me."

"Where is she anyway?" Bostwick asked, wondering how much she'd told his old friend.

"Not sure. She said she had some favor to ask me and told me to wait here and chat with you."

"I think you should leave, Clarence."

"Whatever for?"

"Delilah isn't someone to be trifled with. She seems innocent, and, well, slightly mad, but I think there's more going on here than meets the eye. I don't want her to start collecting any more magicians."

"You haven't changed a bit," said Clarence, unconcerned by Bostwick's warning. "You were always so cautious about everything. I'm sure Delilah means no harm. What gave you such an idea anyway?"

Bostwick looked around conspiratorially, wondering if Delilah might be hiding somewhere, using the Domino to disguise herself as something in the room.

"I'm not serving her because I want to. She has me imprisoned here, as well as a girl named Millicent."

"You must mean the maid. Delilah told me about her. She seems like a lovely person."

"You're not listening, Clarence."

"Ah, speak of the devil!" he said, for Delilah and Millicent had just entered the room.

"Oh no," said Millicent. "I told you to leave! Why didn't you listen?"

"I'm sorry," Clarence said, taking off his hat. "When I put my mind to something, I just can't stop myself. I just had to meet Delilah in person, you see."

"Don't worry," the queen said in a particularly unctuous manner. "He's free to come and go as he wishes. It's not like he tried to steal from me or anything." She paused to shoot Bostwick a nasty look. "Anyway, I was wondering if you could do something for me, Clarence? You see, today just happens to be Millicent's sixteenth birthday, and I would do something special, but as it is, I'm swamped with a bomb scare investigation, not to mention trying to re-grow a trampled and scorched hedge maze. So, if you would be so kind as to take Millicent to the Capital for me, I'd be ever so obliged."

Millicent's eyes nearly popped out of her head.

"You really mean it, Delilah?"

"Of course. You should always mean what you say."

"Very well", said Clarence, putting his hat back onto his head, "to the Capital it is! I just happen to have a vehicle for just this purpose."

He clapped his hands—which was an impressive feat, as he was cradling Jill in one of his arms—and in a poof of blue smoke, a colorful carpet appeared on the floor.

"A magic carpet!" Bostwick gasped. "Where'd you get a thing like that?"

"I picked it up for a song at one of the fine shops in the town. This is in fact a perfect replica of the carpet of Aalem Shariba, winner of five consecutive carpet races across the Nopali Desert. It's quite rare."

"And priceless?"

"Why, yes. How did you know?"

"I don't think you want to be flying on that," Bostwick said. Millicent nodded in agreement.

"Nonsense! I'm sure it will be fine."

Without further ado, he sat on the front end of the carpet and set Jill down next to him. Millicent hesitantly followed suit. After all, they were still on the ground, and if the carpet didn't work, the ground was the safest place to be.

"Carpet, up," Clarence commanded, as if he'd been flying on carpets since birth.

To everyone's surprise, save Clarence's, the carpet rose off the ground.

"Forward."

The carpet lurched backward, sending all its passengers face-forward to the floor.

"I suppose we were sitting on it the wrong way," Clarence said, and clambered back onto the carpet with Jill in his arms. Millicent climbed back on awkwardly and looked back at Delilah as if asking for help. Delilah gave her nothing but a grin and a thumbs-up.

"Okay, carpet. Slowly forward."

It moved to his command, and sailed slowly to the door.

"Well, we'll be off then," he said. "Carpet, away!"

Millicent shrieked as the carpet zoomed down the hallway, through the door, and out the greenhouse window.

Bostwick looked at Delilah, wondering if she'd sent Millicent to her doom. Delilah looked back coldly, with one eyebrow raised, as if to ask Bostwick if he really thought she was that stupid. Then she smiled, putting her hands on her hips.

"Well, what do you know, something of Polkory's actually worked. Now, Bostwick, stop lollygagging and go work on the hedge."

"I thought you said you would be doing that."

"What an idea, Bostwick! I'm too busy making sure you do your work to do any myself. Really, it's so hard to find good help these days."

And with that, she slinked away, leaving Bostwick to wonder why he'd even been called up there in the first place.

Clarence had decided to give Millicent what he called his personalized birthday tour of the entire Capital. They visited museums and gardens and saw the insides of factories. All the while, Clarence told her stories about each place, things he and Bostwick had done while studying at the Academy. He seemed to admire Bostwick a lot.

"He was always sharp as a tack," Clarence told her, as they were walking past the birdcages in the Capital's multi-story zoo, "and had sort of understated flare. This one time, we were learning how to restore broken pocket watches, and most everyone was struggling. This one girl finally gets hers into one piece, though the hands didn't move and the glass was cracked. And she looks over to Bostwick and says, extremely snootily, I might add, 'Beat that, Dogsbody.' But Bostwick just picks up the dust that used to be his watch, pours it into his hat, and says, completely calm, 'It's not a contest,' then pulls out a polished, ticking, good-as-new watch. And then he didn't say anything, didn't have to. He just looked at her."

Millicent smiled. It sounded like the Academy would have been a lot of fun.

"Delilah said you could do magic—is that right?"

Clarence continued.

"What? She said…? Well, it's true. I'm not very good at it, though."

"Show me a spell."

Millicent looked around. It was hardly the time or place, what with so many flammable birds around, but Clarence looked so expectant.

"Well, I have gotten pretty at good one of them," she said. "You wouldn't happen to have a handkerchief on you, would you?"

He handed her one, and she flicked it back and forth in the air three times. With a pop, it turned into a white daisy.

"Marvelous!" Clarence said. "Can you change it back, too?

Millicent did so, and returned the handkerchief to him.

"I know a few other spells, card tricks mostly, but there aren't many that I'm good at."

"—yet," Clarence said matter-of-factly. "Oh look! An exhibit on zebras!"

They continued through the zoo as Clarence prattled on about how he had once tried to ride a zebra through the halls of the Academy, much to Bostwick's consternation. Millicent listened, but was actually wondering if there was not some ulterior motive to her spending the day with Clarence. How much had Delilah really told him?

Bostwick had finally cut and cleared away the damaged foliage from the wyrm incident and was ready to take a well-deserved rest when Emmaline came hopping up to him.

"Delilah wants to see you."

Bostwick looked at his dirt-covered clothes and scratched hands.

"Can I at least get cleaned up first?"

"She insisted you do."

After Bostwick had washed up and changed clothes, he went to find Delilah, who was lounging sideways on her throne. When she noticed him, she threw her hands up dramatically.

"*Bost*wick! It's terrible! Awful! Urgent!"

"But not urgent enough for me to show up all covered in dirt?" Bostwick asked, only somewhat sarcastically.

"We are civilized here, Bostwick. Cleanliness is next to godliness, and to forgive is divine, so do forgive me if I say that haste makes waste, and waste is dirty."

Bostwick blinked, dumbstruck.

"Moving on. I feel I have made a terrible error in judgment, allowing Millie to go off to a large city with a man I barely know! Oh me, oh my, oh what's to be done? Bostwick, you must rescue her!"

"Rescue her?"

"At this very moment, Clarence may be beguiling her with his masculine wiles. Something must be done!"

"Clarence isn't that kind of person," Bostwick said, though he felt sure it was useless.

"Perhaps, but surely his good looks and charming personality will steal her heart away, even by accident."

"Maybe," Bostwick said, considering it, "but that might not be a bad thing. They're both good people, and their personalities actually seem to suit each other. They might run into financial trouble, seeing as they're both, well you know."

Delilah's grip on her chair tightened and she gritted her teeth.

"You're hopeless, Bostwick. Look, just get the car and go."

"Even if I did go, which I'm not saying I will, how would I find them? The Capital's huge."

"They should be dining at Exupéry's Restaurant. That's what I told Clarence to do anyway."

"Told him? Wait a minute, you don't have some sort of scheme going on in that goblin head of yours?"

She relaxed, returning to her lazy, sideways position again.

"A goblin who isn't scheming isn't doing his job. Speaking of which…" she said with an impish grin. "Be aware that if you get any funny ideas about escaping while you're there, I'll know, and I'll curse you so badly that your grandchildren will feel it, assuming you have any."

"You don't need to tell me that," he grumbled, secretly surprised that escape hadn't even crossed his mind. "Besides, Emmaline is still here, so it's not like I can leave her behind."

"Hmm, I suppose not. Anyway, you'll need to get a move on. I want Millie back before nightfall. The woods are winding and difficult to navigate at night. During the day, too, but you can't see in the dark, now can you? Hmm, better bring the cat just in case."

Bostwick supposed it was better than working on the garden, so he quickly went to find Sebastian and be on his way. The cat turned out to be wandering around the treasure chamber, and seemed slightly disturbed when Bostwick told him about their task.

"The Capital? Why does she want me to go?"

"Apparently you can see in the dark and we'll be traveling at night or something. I wouldn't complain. This means we'll have an entire evening devoid of Delilah."

The cat still seemed reluctant, but silently followed Bostwick to the garden. When they arrived at the outside ramada they did not find the jaunty car, but instead a shiny, purple, metal contraption without any harness or yoke in front. Delilah sat proudly in the front seat, holding a long scarf, gloves, and goggles.

"Surprised?" she asked, opening the side door and stepping down.

"What is it?" Sebastian asked, sniffing one of the wheels.

"An automobile: a machine on the cutting edge of technology. I received it as a present some months ago, but was saving it until the right moment. Here." she said, shoving the assortment of accessories into Bostwick's arms. "Put them on. You'll look ever so much more dashing this way, and you won't get as filthy, either."

Bostwick did as he was told simply to avoid an argument. It seemed Delilah was in a rare form of insanity today. He and Sebastian got into the vehicle, but could not figure out what to do next. There was a helm for steering, as one might find on a ship, as well as a lever, and several pedals on the floor.

"So… how does it go?" Bostwick asked.

"On its own of course. What do you think 'automobile' means? Or did you mean how to start it?"

She ran to the front of the car and inserted a long, zigzagging piece of metal into the grille, then cranked it around and around. Something inside the automobile made a crunching, growling noise, then a sound like an explosion, and the machine began to inch forward, barely giving her time to get out of the way.

"Now, remember," she said, tossing the piece of metal into the back seat, "left goes left and right goes right. And one of the floor pedals is a brake."

"Wait," said Bostwick, as the car began to pick up speed, "which pedal, and what about this lever? How do I make it go slower?"

"I don't know," Delilah called, as the car sped out the gate and into the forest.

As it turned out, Exupéry's was as fancy a restaurant as Millicent had ever been in. Crystal chandeliers hung from the high ceiling, on which romantic pastel scenes were painted. The maître d' had refused to let them in at first, even though Millicent had wisely removed her apron before entering and looked moderately well dressed without it. Clarence, on the other hand, still had his shabby tailcoat and soon-to-be-topless hat, as well as a live jackalope in his arms. Only when he explained about his very distant relationship to the empress herself, aided by a family tree he happened to be carrying with him, was he allowed to enter, though the maitre d' insisted he leave Jill and his hat at the front desk.

"This place is very nice, but isn't it sort of expensive?" Millicent observed, not being as fiscally injudicious as Bostwick thought.

"Delilah gave me money. After all, this whole ordeal is

really her birthday gift to you. I was just a convenient means of delivering it."

"So that *was* her plan."

"Hmm?" Clarence purred, sounding very much like Delilah herself.

"Oh, I was just thinking. This whole trip seemed sort of suspicious, too much for a simple present."

"Well, I was also told to say something to Bostwick when he comes here to get you. Apparently he's been moping around the castle lately. Any idea why?"

Millicent thought, finishing her stuffed mushrooms.

"He has been sort of gloomy. I think he really does hate working for Delilah, when he could've gone back to being a court magician. I've tried convincing her to let him go, but she refuses. She says it's because he tried to steal the Domino from her, but…"

She stopped. Clarence was looking at her with a strange expression, somewhere between confusion and amusement.

"Gosh, I probably shouldn't have told you about that!" she said. "Bostwick really isn't a thief. I suppose he did try to take Delilah's mask, but that was to help Emmaline. He's a good person!" Clarence looked more amused by the second, but Millicent was trying to make her point as clear as possible. "You said it yourself, how he's smart and modest, and he tried to follow the rules at the Academy, and I don't think that one act of thievery should seal his fate as a criminal!"

Clarence burst out laughing, as a nearby waiter shot him a disdainful glance.

"You're very good at defending people, I'll give you that, but I know Bostwick's no criminal. Well, technically he is, but that doesn't mean he's a bad guy. And I think Delilah knows that too. But you were saying maybe she had some other reason for keeping him around?"

Millicent was about to reply, but Clarence waved to someone behind her.

"Hello, Bostwick. What are you doing here?"

Bostwick stood there, wearing a scarf and goggles, looking extremely shaken.

"Delilah sent me to come get Millicent. I took the automobile," he added grimly.

"Really?" Millicent asked, forgetting the conversation from a moment ago. "Delilah said she was saving that for a special occasion. This is the best birthday ever!"

"I don't wish to delay your departure," Clarence said, "but could I quickly borrow Bostwick before you go?"

"Of course."

Millicent excused herself and Bostwick took her chair.

"What is it?"

"You're a lucky man, Bostwick."

"Eh?" This was the only way he could respond to such a bizarre, out-of-the-blue comment.

"You're lucky, that's all. The way things have turned out for you... I'm glad. Everyone always wondered if you'd be all right, unable to be the best magician that you could be, but I always knew you'd show them."

"I'm no better than the rest of them," Bostwick said, embarrassed by such lavish praise.

"That Millicent's got potential, though," Clarence continued, somehow managing to sound sly and innocent at the same time, "for magic, I mean."

"I think so, too," Bostwick replied, though he wondered how Clarence knew about that.

"Then there's nothing else for it!" He leapt up from the table and clapped Bostwick on the shoulder. "If she's going to learn magic, then she's got to be taught magic!"

"Yes, that's generally how—"

"And you shall teach her!"

"What?"

Bostwick threw off his friend's hand and fell sideways out of his chair, to the stares of the other restaurant patrons.

"You're the only one for the job, Bostwick. She needs you! It's her dream. Don't you want to help her fulfill her dream? Only a true magician can train another, and you, my friend, are a true magician."

"But I don't know the first thing about how to teach someone else," he said, standing up. "I can't even remember the first spell I ever did."

"Piffle, the past is past, why dwell on it? In the future lives a girl who needs your help, and a hundred years or so in which you are imprisoned with her. It could be a nice way to pass the time."

"But what if I can't do it?" Bostwick asked, though somehow Clarence's words about the past had already consoled him.

"Nonsense! I have complete faith in you." He dropped a stack of bills on the table, then walked to the doorway and grabbed Jill and his hat. "Well, it was nice seeing you, my old friend, but now I'm off to see the world. Good luck!"

With that he ran out the door and disappeared.

Eight

The Forest of Infinite Horrors

Millicent found Sebastian outside waiting in the automobile. He was turning his head this way and that, staring at everything around him. He was so absorbed in watching a couple of people walk past that he didn't even notice Millicent approach.

"It might kill you," she said.

Sebastian turned to her, startled.

"Being curious," she said smiling. "You know what they say about cats. Although Delilah says goblins consider curiosity to be a virtue."

"The human saying is more accurate."

"Let's go," Bostwick said, coming out of the restaurant. He was looking at Millicent with a strange expression, almost like he was appraising her.

"What's the matter?"

"Nothing," he said, grabbing the zigzagging metal bar from the back seat. "You'd better get in. I don't know how soon this thing will start up."

He put the bar into a hole in the front of the and turned it several times, but nothing happened.

"Perhaps it got broken when we hit that sign post," Sebastian offered.

"I know," said Millicent, clapping her hands. "Delilah told me that what makes this machine run on its own is a special kind of fuel burning, like in an oil lamp. I bet it's all out of it, since you came all the way from Styx. We just need to get some more."

They looked around them. Everywhere, there were horse-drawn wagons and carriages, and the occasional rickshaw, but nowhere else were there any automobiles. Bostwick doubted that automobile oil would be the sort of thing one could walk down the street and buy.

"So much for the cutting edge of technology," he said. "I guess we could get one of the taximeter cabs to take us back. Delilah can foot the bill."

Bostwick flagged down one of the horse-drawn cabs, as Millicent and Sebastian were unacquainted with the use of taximeters. When one finally stopped, Bostwick asked how much it would cost to go to Styx Castle.

"Are you pig-licking insane? I wouldn't go through the Forest of Infinite Horrors if you plated my carriage in gold and me with it."

"But we just came through there this afternoon."

"Well, I suppose in the day the horrors might be sleeping or something, but no one who doesn't like serpents and monsters goes in there at night."

With that, he flicked the reins and went on his way.

"We'll have to walk, then," Sebastian said

♠ ♦ ♣ ♥ ♣ ♦ ♠

The edge of the forest was not so terrible, Bostwick thought, nor was it when he'd driven through it earlier, though he hadn't really had time to look around him as he was busy avoiding trees and boulders. As they went along, however, the trees got thicker and thicker, obscuring the moonlight from above and tripping their feet from below. Bostwick snapped his fingers and created a small flame, but it was difficult to see very far ahead. He suggested that Millicent try the same spell, but she adamantly refused, insisting that she might start the whole forest on fire around them. They continued on in near darkness. Sebastian went swiftly forward, as if the path was clear, while the humans stumbled over rocks and fallen branches.

"You know, Millicent," Bostwick began, ducking under a low-hanging branch, "I could teach you the fire spell."

"It's too dangerous."

"Well, what about when we get back to the castle?"

Millicent tripped over a log.

"Really?" she asked, picking herself up.

"Sure. And I could show you other spells, too. What I mean is, why don't I teach you magic? Just because you didn't get to study at the Academy doesn't mean you can't be a true magician. What do you say?"

In response, she made a strange squealing noise that Bostwick had heard many of the female students at the Academy make when Clarence did something spectacularly clumsy or stupid.

"So, that's a 'yes'?"

"Yes, yes, yes!" she cried. "Oh, Bostwick! Thank you so much. We should start as soon as we get back!"

"Well, maybe we should wait till tomorrow."

"All right!"

"You might want to keep your voices down," said Sebastian. "We don't want to attract any creatures."

"Lighten up," Bostwick said. "We haven't seen anything except trees and mushrooms all night."

"You haven't, but I can see things moving. Crawling, creeping, slithering things."

"Big things?" Millicent asked, picking up a club-like branch for self defense.

"Sometimes it doesn't matter if it's big, if there are lots of whatever it is."

The humans looked into the darkness of the forest, searching for claws and teeth they could not see. Then they heard it: a strange scuffling noise going on all around them, and a sound like scales sliding through fallen leaves.

"So, what sorts of things are supposed to live in here anyway?" Millicent asked. Apparently, for all her knowledge of Styx, she knew little about its forest.

"I've heard some stories," Bostwick said, "but I doubt most of them are true. Some say the plants themselves can move and talk. Others say there's some sort of creature called a grudge that's supposed to strangle you or something. Mostly, though, the forest is famous for its snakes."

"Snakes!"

Millicent looked at her feet, as if an army of snakes was waiting to coil up around her.

"They're just stories, though" he assured her. "Since no one goes into this forest, no one really knows. And if it *is* only snakes, we just have to watch our feet."

At that very moment, something slammed into his head. He looked around for what it was, and on the ground saw a small green snake shaking itself. It looked at Bostwick, then turned, rose into the air, and glided away.

"Did that snake just fly?" Bostwick asked, rubbing his head.

"Apparently so," said Sebastian. "Watch your feet *and* your heads from now on."

As they went further, they saw many more snakes flying through the air, as well as other serpents going about their nightly business. Some rolled in hoops while others slithered sideways. Occasionally, they would see giant coils, thick as tree trunks, going through the trees with no head or tail in sight. They saw one snake that glowed blue and emitted a high pitched scream, similar to a human voice. Millicent held her tree branch closer to her, terrified of the reptilian wonders that surrounded them. Bostwick was much calmer.

"For a place called 'The Forest of Infinite Horrors', this isn't very horrible."

"You aren't scared?"

"No. These snakes aren't even doing anything. Sure, they're pretty bizarre," he said, watching one snake expand and contract like a bull frog throat, "but they aren't hurting us. I don't even think they care we're here."

"True," Sebastian said, "but what about those other things you mentioned? The walking trees and that strangulation monster?"

"They obviously aren't real." He bent down to a knee-high, purple spotted mushroom as wide as a lady's sun hat and poked its stem. "See, this thing isn't moving, it's just—"

Before he could finish, the cap of the mushroom shot downward like an umbrella closing and engulfed Bostwick's arm almost to the elbow. He cried out, for the cap was edged with sharp teeth and was covered, he saw, not in white spots but eyes that were looking hungrily up at him.

"I'm stuck," he said. "Do something!"

Sebastian approached the mushroom and scratched it, but it did not release Bostwick. Millicent ran forward and observed the fungus, then poked it hard in the eye. The mushroom blinked its eyes and opened its cap, allowing Bostwick to remove his arm, which was covered in blood and sticky slime.

"Thanks. What on earth was that, anyway?"

"A carnivorous mushroom," Millicent said. "They're the kind we use in bat-mushroom stew. I didn't recognize it alive, or I would've warned you."

Bostwick rolled up his sleeve to inspect the wound more closely. Blood was still flowing from deep, jagged bite marks.

"Not good. I can't heal this without a box, and it doesn't look like it's going to stop anytime soon."

"I've heard the mushroom's slime makes things bleed faster," Millicent said.

Sebastian observed the wound thoughtfully, then looked at Millicent, who was already tearing strips off her apron for a makeshift bandage.

"Can't you do something?" he asked, sounding more curious than concerned.

"Like what?"

It was a while before the cat responded.

"Try making the blood he's lost return to his body. Do

you know how?"

Millicent thought for a bit. She wouldn't have wanted to do magic in a place like this, but it seemed necessary. Besides, she'd practiced this spell with success many times when cleaning up spills. She held her left hand over Bostwick's wound, and began to recite:

"Flowing essence, end this pain.

Needless bleeding, cease your flood.

Trickle back within the vein.

Pulse again, oh dark life's blood."

The blood ran up Bostwick's arm as it would down a waterfall. Bostwick clenched his teeth, as the sensation of blood coming back into his veins was not a pleasant one. Millicent quickly bandaged the wound before it had a chance to start bleeding again.

"Where did you learn a spell like that?" Bostwick asked, astounded. He flexed his arm to make sure the bandages would stay in place.

"It was written in one of those books I studied back home."

"Impressive," Sebastian whispered.

"I've never heard a chant for a spell like that before," Bostwick said.

"There are other types of magic humans can do," Sebastian said, and slinked past Millicent's feet, "although it's interesting that you can do it. You know, I know a bit about human magic; I could help teach you, along with Bostwick."

"All right," Millicent said, petting Sebastian's head. "I really am lucky, you know. This morning was just another day, and now, I'm another year older, I've been all over the

Capital, and have two people to teach me magic. Nothing can spoil this day!"

Nothing except a blood-curdling howl they heard behind them, and a crash, like a tree being rent from the ground and cracking downward.

"I say we run for it," Bostwick suggested.

The others agreed, and did so.

"War!" Delilah said with glee, and placed three cards face down beside her three of hearts, then turned over one more card revealing a jack of clubs, "Mwahaha! Beat that!"

"King," Emmaline said, flipping over a king of clubs.

"No fair! No fair! I only have two cards left."

"You could still turn it around," the rabbit said, sliding her winnings over to her pile with her paws. "My tea inspector once won the whole deck back with only an ace of diamonds. Of course, you won't be so lucky."

Delilah slapped a mosquito away and straightened her pitiful card pile. She and Emmaline sat on the steps of the castle under the glow of lantern light.

"I can't concentrate with all these bugs. That's why I'm losing."

"You wanted to wait out here for them to come back. We can go inside if you want."

"No! We must wait for them. It's our duty as friends. Ha! A seven!"

"A ten."

Delilah bit her lip, peeking at her final card.

"Curse you humans and your cursed human card games.

This is all luck! There is no skill involved."

"We can play Crazy Eights," Emmaline said, flipping over a four of hearts.

"So close," the queen said, flicking her last card, a three, at Emmaline. "You've won this round. But you'd better watch your back from now on. Oh, look! There they are."

Millicent and Sebastian trudged slowly up the path toward them; there were a few leaves in their hair. Bostwick came last, limping badly. His clothes were torn and covered in mud, he had a black eye and a bandaged arm, and a strange furry creature clung by the teeth to his ankle.

"Hello," Delilah called. "So how was the Capital?"

"It was," Millicent panted, "nice."

"And the trip back was fine?"

"It was a veritable nightmare," Sebastian said coldly, "or have you never been through the Forest of Infinite Horrors?"

"Oh, that old thing. It's just a name, the same way 'Sebastian' is just a name. From now on, I shall refer to you as Sir Alowhiskers Bartholomeow Von Meowinstein the Third, since you've decided to stay here."

"How is *that*," Bostwick gasped, pointing back toward the forest, "just a name?"

"Well, way back when, my ancestors decided that they didn't want humans popping by every few seconds, so they dubbed it 'The Forest of Infinite Horrors' to keep people away. Really, it's a lovely place full of adorable woodland creatures."

"Lovely? I would maybe, *maybe* say that the snakes were lovely, in that they didn't attack us. But then I got bitten by a mushroom, which shouldn't be possible, then we got chased by this huge bird-monster-thing, then I fell in mud, which turned out to be quicksand, and when I got out, we saw this weird glowing light far away that we thought was the castle. So we followed the light, which turned out to be some sort of will-o-wisp that led us right to a cave full of—my favorite—wyrms. So we had to run from them, downhill, in the dark, which is where this happened," he said, indicating his eye. "That forest is the most *horrible* place I've ever been."

"It was pretty bad, Delilah," Millicent said.

"What about that thing?" Emmaline asked, indicating the creature on Bostwick's ankle.

"Oh, this?" he said, prying the creature off. "Yeah, so when I finally thought we were in the clear, this dropped on me and wrapped these," he held up the creatures limp, stringy arms, "around my throat. I thought I'd gotten rid of it back there."

"They're very hard to get rid of." Delilah said. "The creature you hold in your hands is called a grudge. They'll latch on and never let go if you aren't careful. Apparently the man who named them liked to be didactic."

Bostwick dropped the creature unceremoniously on the ground, where it rolled into the hedge maze.

"I'm healing my arm, then going to bed," he said, and went into the castle.

"I suppose that'll do for now," Delilah said. "I still haven't decided what he'll be doing tomorrow."

"About that," said Millicent. "Bostwick offered to teach me magic—he and Sebastian. Can't we put off cleaning for just a little while? The castle's mostly livable now, and we just won't go into the dirty parts. All right?"

"Hmm, I suppose. Yes," she said smiling, "Bostwick will teach you magic. We shall set aside time every afternoon for just this purpose. An excellent idea. But I still feel as if something isn't quite right about this. Something's missing… Where's the car?"

Nine

Tarts, Trifles, and Tricks

"So how are magic lessons going?" Delilah asked, handing Millicent a long wire whisk.

"I'm getting better and better. Look."

Millicent took a card from her pocket and flicked it several times. The card changed from the three of clubs to the ace of spades to the queen of hearts, then disappeared in a puff of smoke.

"Ooh!" Delilah said.

"And yesterday, Bostwick showed me how to levitate a book. I can get it a few inches off the ground, but I still have trouble controlling it. But Bostwick said that's perfectly normal for first year students."

"Ah, so he's going year by year, as you would in school. Silly."

"Silly?" Millicent asked, whisking the contents of a large bowl. She and Delilah were in the kitchen baking. Specifically, Millicent was making several different varieties of cookies, tarts, and scones, while Delilah handed her ingredients and cooking utensils.

"You humans and your organization. Always classifying

spells. I'll never understand it. For example, what on earth is the difference between a spell, a trick, and a charm?"

Millicent shrugged.

"See, you don't even understand it yourselves. Back in my day, magic was magic and we liked it that way."

"But putting things in lists makes them easier to remember. Like the different kinds of spells and the different props you need for them. Bostwick made a chart for me. And then he told me the rules about what sort of items you can vanish and conjure back. Really, I think he's a much better teacher than whoever wrote those books I was using before."

"In all fairness, the books were probably written for the author's own use, not for instruction."

"I guess. But I still think Bostwick knows more about magic. Like how the spells in those books were always cast one-handed, but Bostwick says that most spells don't work that way and the author was just being lazy."

"In all fairness," Delilah said again, "the author may have been an amputee, or maybe they were always carrying a baby in one arm."

"Maybe," Millicent laughed, "but I've learned three times as many spells from Bostwick than I learned from those books, and we've only been practicing for a month."

"In all fairness, maybe that's because you're madly in love with him."

"I am not," Millicent said, blushing and looking around wildly.

"Don't worry; he can't hear us. He's still cleaning out the dungeon, far, far below."

As punishment for leaving Delilah's automobile in the

Capital, Bostwick had been ordered to clean every inch of the honeycomb-like dungeons. Even after the car had been returned, showing up mysteriously one morning, Delilah demanded he finish the job.

"It wasn't his fault about the car," Millicent insisted. "He didn't know it needed fuel. You never told him."

"I know, but those dungeons really must be clean for when we catch the mad bomber."

"How's the case coming, anyway?" Millicent said, trying to move the subject away from her feelings for Bostwick.

"Nine more bombs have shown up, all of them duds. I wish Heather could put up some sort of sign telling the bomber that they can't blow up Styx that way. It's such a nuisance. Speaking of which, next time you see Whiskers McFluffy, could you tell him that?"

"Sebastian's not the mad bomber," Millicent said adamantly.

"That may be so, but why does he keep hanging around the castle?"

"Maybe he has nowhere else to go. Could you hand me the sugar?"

"Well, he should at least pay rent or do dishes or something."

"He's helping me with magic."

"That's acceptable, I suppose," Delilah said, plunking down an enormous glass jar filled with sugar, "but why do you need *his* help?"

"He doesn't teach the same way as Bostwick. He says I should work on the spells I already know and try to remember as much from those books as possible. And he explains the spells really strangely."

"Well of course. Goblins don't cast human spells. Remember when I tried to explain how to light a card on fire?"

"You said to get angry at it."

"Yes," Delilah smiled, as if her explanation was the cleverest thing anyone had ever said.

"Bostwick says you have to will the card and the air around it to combust at the same time."

Delilah looked confused and said, "Well, sure, but it's easier to get angry at something, because when you're mad at it, you want it to burst into flames. Doesn't that make perfect sense?"

"I guess so. You and Bostwick are basically saying the same things, but Sebastian's different. I was telling him about this spell for fixing broken glass; it was one of the ones from the books, and he really seemed to understand it. He told me how to focus on the unbroken form of the glass itself and use magic to bind the pieces into that form by thinking of where each piece should go. And when I did, the jar I broke came right back together like new! It was amazing."

"Hmm," was all Delilah said.

Millicent hurried over to one of the large ovens in the wall and took out a tray of lemon tarts.

"What are all of these things for, anyway?" Delilah asked.

"I wanted to thank them for teaching me, so I baked for them. Everyone likes food."

"It's true," Delilah agreed, "and the way to a man's heart is through his stomach."

"Well, that, too," Millicent said, smiling.

♠ ♦ ♣ ♥ ♣ ♦ ♠

Not knowing when Bostwick would be finished in the dungeons, Millicent decided to find Sebastian first.

"He's in the hall of portraits," said Emmaline, whom Millicent almost tripped over when coming out of the kitchen. "Can I have one of those scones?"

"Of course." She lifted Emmaline up to ride on her shoulder and handed her a piece of scone. "Have you found out anything yet about the curse?"

Emmaline had been poring over library books for the past few days, after Millicent had gotten them down to rabbit-level for her and Sebastian had given her some tips for turning pages with her paws.

"After flipping through *Flora, Fauna, and Fungi of the Goblin World*, I now know that my attacker was a long-tailed imp," Emmaline said, nibbling on the scone, "which I think I could have figured out on my own. Other than that, I haven't found much."

"I wish I could do something for you, but all the spells I know are just for everyday things."

"It's all right. I've been a rabbit for over year now; I don't think a few more weeks of searching will hurt anything."

They soon found Sebastian in the hall of portraits, staring up at the painting of the large garden party. His eyes were narrowed, which gave him a pensive look, even though it was hard to tell with cats.

"Hello, Sebastian," Millicent said, approaching him.

"Hello."

He did not look at her as he spoke. Emmaline wondered

if maybe they should leave, as he seemed to be in an untalkative mood.

"Um, I brought you something." Millicent produced a tin filled with baked goods, pink confetti, and ribbon; Delilah had insisted that presentation was key. "They're a thank you present for teaching me magic."

Sebastian sniffed the tin experimentally.

"Thank you," he said, sounding fairly surprised, "but I don't know if I'll be able to eat this."

Millicent's smile disintegrated.

"Oh no! It's because you're a cat, right? I should've thought of that. Maybe I can make, um, chicken flavored cake… with tuna frosting. That could be good."

"Why don't you try eating some of it?" Emmaline addressed Sebastian, who looked politely disgusted at the idea of tuna frosting. "I've always been able to eat regular food, despite being a rabbit. It's the magic of the curse, I guess."

Sebastian hesitated, but took a bite of the lemon tart. He swallowed, then closed his eyes, looking actually happy.

"It's good," he said. "I've never had lemon tart before. I never imagined a sour fruit actually tasting good, but it is. But where did you get a lemon? Aren't they hard to come by?"

"They grow in an underground garden with the pineapples," Millicent said. "We have lots of them."

Sebastian looked intrigued and ate another bite.

"These were a delicacy where I came from," he said. "Only the richest people had ever seen a lemon, let alone tasted one."

"Where are you from?" Emmaline asked. She'd been curious about Sebastian ever since Bostwick had first told her about him. He was too secretive and his story too suspicious. Even now, he waited several seconds before responding.

"My people live far to the west of here."

Millicent, who had very little grasp of geography, nodded. Emmaline, however, began picturing a world map in her head.

"So what kind of goblin were you?"

"You wouldn't have heard of us," he said simply.

"I can't help but imagine," Millicent said, "that you would have great white whiskers and big ears and maybe a large stomach."

Sebastian laughed a silky, smirking laugh that was quite similar to Delilah's.

"I'm afraid you'll be sorely disappointed when you see my true form. If I ever get it back," he added bitterly.

"Don't worry. I'm sure you'll both find a way to break your curses. I don't know about yours, Emmaline, but if the Styx goblins were the ones who cursed you, Sebastian, then Delilah can probably break it."

"Even if she could, she wouldn't," Sebastian said, looking back to the painting on the wall. "Styx goblins don't help people unless they get something in return."

"You should give Delilah a chance," Millicent said. "She only acts like she doesn't care because she thinks it's funny. I bet if you asked her to break the curse, she'd do it."

"You give her too much credit; all of you humans do. Why do you like the Styx goblins so much, anyway?"

"What do you mean?"

"I can see admiring them if you'd never met them and they seemed to you to be…" and here he paused, as if trying to think of the right word, "…exotic. But to know how cruel and manipulative they are and still hold them in high regard? That makes no sense to me."

"She's really not *that* manipulative," Millicent said.

At that very moment, Delilah called loudly from the floor below.

"Why, Bostwick, you're back from the dungeon! Don't you look smashing, all covered in dirt. If only Millicent were here to see you. She was looking for you."

"Ah! I'm coming!" Millicent cried, and dashed away to stop Delilah from saying anything more embarrassing.

Emmaline stayed. She looked over the portrait that Sebastian seemed to be absorbed in: the diverse group of goblins, the one with the long braid, and the man with the beard. Then she looked at Sebastian, who had an expression of disgust on his face, while his tail twitched angrily.

"What's wrong?" she asked.

"I really despise them," he said simply.

"Them?" She glanced at the painting, which Sebastian had not taken his eyes off of. "You mean you actually knew *them*?"

Sebastian twitched and looked at her, his expression unfathomable.

"Don't be ridiculous. I don't know a single one of those particular people," he said, although he glanced at the braid-wearing goblin. "I only meant Styx goblins in general. But all goblins hate Styx. Who wouldn't?"

He seemed almost embarrassed and began to wash his front paw, as if that would change the subject. Since he didn't seem to want to talk any further, Emmaline hopped away.

That night, she contemplated what the cat had said, and what he had refused to say. She had a theory, but it seemed crazy. Then again, she'd seen many crazy things on her travels through Ataxia.

The next day, she went to find Delilah, who was in one of the bedrooms upstairs directing Bostwick on how to hang some new wallpaper, as she had finally given him a reprieve from dungeon duty.

"That looks straight," the queen said, "but we're goblins, aren't we? Tilt it a little more to the left. A bit more. There, that's just subtle enough to be annoying but not enough to really be noticeable. Perfect. Oh, hello, Emmaline. Have you come to help, too?"

"Actually, I was wondering if I could have word with you. Alone."

"Don't want the rabble in on it, eh," she whispered, looking at Bostwick.

"You know I can hear you," he said.

"Listening in, eh? Well, it's no more than I would expect from your sort."

"My sort?" Bostwick asked, beginning to get angry, but Emmaline spoke before he could get a chance.

"Please, Delilah. It's sort of important."

The two of them went out into the next bedroom and shut the door.

"You know how Sebastian is helping teach Millicent magic," Emmaline began, "and how he just wanders around the castle? Well, don't you think that's a little dangerous?"

"How so?"

"For all we know, he could be the bomber, and furthermore, I was talking to him yesterday, and he's just been acting strangely, and well…"

"Go on."

"Have you ever heard of… immortal beasts?"

"What about them?"

She faltered, already knowing how ridiculous it would sound out loud.

"Do you think Sebastian could be an immortal beast?"

Delilah put her hand beneath her chin and thought it over.

"Well, he has lived abnormally long for a cat. He always used to ask me about what was going on in the world, saying he had no idea how much time had passed since he was imprisoned. And my mother couldn't remember ever having put him in the dungeon either. Hmm."

"But then, what does he want?" Emmaline asked. "He obviously has a grudge against Styx for turning him into a cat. So why is he being so friendly all of a sudden, and why does he want to teach Millicent magic?"

"You don't trust him?"

"I don't. There's just something about him that seems wrong, almost out of place. Out of place with humans and out of place with Styx."

"If you suspect him," Delilah said, kneeling down to be more near Emmaline's height, "why not spy on him, hmm? You can just sneak, sneak, sneak, on your little bunny feet, into the tower where he sleeps and check it out. I think you're the perfect candidate. You're small, you're quiet, and best of all, if you do get caught, you can make up some sob story about how he's the only one in your same situation and how you thought he'd understand."

"That's not a bad idea. How do you come up with these things?"

"I'm a goblin queen. It's in my blood."

"I think you should practice levitation again today," Bostwick said, vanishing a wad of paste that had stuck to his sleeve. After they had finished cleaning for the day, he and Millicent met Sebastian in the upstairs library to practice magic tricks.

"Okay." Millicent picked a book from the shelf and placed it on the table, then held her hand, palm up, beside it. She held her breath and brought her hand up slowly. As she did so, the book rose three inches off the tabletop. It shook slightly in the air, but remained at a constant height.

"You don't have to hold your breath," Sebastian said, jumping onto the table.

Millicent exhaled and the book sank back down,

"Just think of it like a heavier deck of cards," Bostwick said.

"I can only levitate a few cards at a time, though."

"I know, but a similar principle is involved. And you can already move cards through the air, so it seems like you're already pretty skilled in levitation. You just need to work with bigger objects. This time, I want you to keep the book steady."

Millicent nodded and once more levitated the book

several inches off the table. It tilted from side to side, so she held her hand as still as she could. Nothing changed.

"It's all right if you move a little," Bostwick said. "Just stay calm and will the book to do what you want."

"Think of the air as a table," Sebastian suggested. "Lay the book flat on it."

Millicent attempted to, and remembered something she had read in one of her magic books. *It is a fundamental mistake to think of levitation as moving through empty space. Even the air exists invisibly around us.*

Millicent tried to picture setting the book down without actually setting it *down*. The book stopped tilting and began to merely shudder.

"Good," Bostwick said. "See if you can keep it a little more steady."

Millicent nodded, trying to will the book to actually sit on the air. It continued to shake. She squinted at it and stretched her fingers farther apart, willing every ounce of magical power out into her hands. The book stopped moving and sat motionless in midair.

"I got it," she said, staying perfectly still.

"Yeah," Bostwick said, "though you might have over-exerted yourself a little."

Millicent looked at the book, confused.

"Your hair," Sebastian supplied.

Letting the book drop, Millicent grabbed a strand of her hair and held it in front of her eyes. It had turned a mousy brown.

"Oh no!" she said, her eyes widening.

"It's nothing to worry about," Sebastian said. "Magic, as

powerful as it is, still has some limitations. You might have been trying to use so much energy to levitate that book that the spell keeping your hair green failed. The more you practice, the more spells you'll be able to control at once."

"R-right," she said, unconsoled by his explanation.

"Here," Bostwick said, holding his hands several inches from her hair. Millicent froze, wondering simultaneously what Bostwick was doing and why she couldn't stand this still while doing magic.

"There," he said a moment later. "Did I get the shade right?"

Millicent glanced sideways and found that he had turned her hair back to its usual green.

"Y-yeah," she said. "Thanks."

"Oh," Sebastian said, between licks of his paw, "I didn't realize you were upset about the hair itself."

"That's okay. I was just worried that I wouldn't be able to get the color back. I'm a little particular about it."

"Well, it is your favorite spell," Bostwick said.

"*That* spell is?" Sebastian said, laying one ear flat in bewilderment.

"It's not just the spell," Bostwick said, coming to Millicent's defense. "I'm sure it also has to do with it being her first, and also with the hair itself. A lot of human sentiment is focused on hair, and the effect 'Upon the soul with dreamy grace—of woman's hair, the theme of poet's song, in every time and place.'"

Sebastian and Millicent stared at him.

"I-it's just something I read once," he said, straightening his collar distractedly.

"You like poetry, Bostwick?" Millicent asked with a smile.

"No," he said quickly, and snatched up the book they were practicing with. "Talking about hair just reminded me of it. Anyway, after levitation, I can show you how to change the color of objects. It's useful for a lot of things, not just hair. You can practice on handkerchiefs."

"Okay," Millicent said, taking the book in one hand and twisting a strand of hair in the other.

Meanwhile, Emmaline had Delilah bring her to the room where Sebastian spent his nights. It was high up in one of the towers, and it would've taken her all day to get there on her own.

"Good luck," Delilah said, leaving Emmaline outside the wooden door, behind which was the only room in the tower. It opened with a creak, and within, she saw a room that must have been unoccupied for years, and had certainly never been cleaned by Millicent. There was a layer of dust on every surface, sometimes displaced, probably by Sebastian walking or sitting on it. There was almost no furniture in the room—only an empty bookshelf and a low stool, as well as dingy, moth-eaten curtains hanging on either side of the window. Nor was there much in the way of clues, as far as she could see. Now that she was up here, there was no way to get down easily, so she decided to stay and employ Delilah's plan of pretending to confide in Sebastian to try and learn his secrets. She watched the sky outside darken and planned what she would say. Finally, he came climbing up the steps and stopped when he saw Emmaline waiting outside his room.

"Hi, Sebastian," she began.

"What, did Delilah send you up here to spy on me?"

Emmaline faltered, all of her carefully planned words made useless.

"Yes and no. She wants to know what you're up to. But I, well, I'm curious about you, too. You're always talking to Millicent and Bostwick, and I'm out of the loop."

She tried to sound as innocent as possible. She'd often heard her tea inspector negotiating deals with other countries, so she knew what being economical with the truth sounded like.

"Is that so?" Sebastian said, apparently believing her. "Well, I suppose you can come in, then."

He went into his room and jumped onto the windowsill.

"So this is where you sleep, huh?" Emmaline said, as if she hadn't been staring at this room for at least an hour. "I guess it is the second highest place in the castle. Goblins like being high up, right?"

"I don't believe in all that nonsense," Sebastian said. "I like the view, is all."

"The view?"

Sebastian leapt down from his perch and pushed the wooden stool closer so Emmaline could climb up on it. When she reached the windowsill, she looked out. The full moon was in the southeastern sky, and the trees and hedges in the garden stood out eerily against the moon shadows cast beneath them. Far to the south, a cluster of bright lights lit up the night around them.

"Is that the Capital?" Emmaline asked, amazed. "I didn't know you could see it from here. It really is beautiful, but..."

"What?" Sebastian asked, still staring out the window.

"It's full of humans. Why do you like us so much?"

"I don't. I simply think Styxian culture is too ridiculous to admire in any way, while humans… I suppose I find it easier to relate to them."

"Why?"

Sebastian leapt from the window to the dusty shelf next to him.

"You're a curious one, aren't you?"

"Sorry!" she said, worried that she'd asked too much.

"It's all right. It's only natural to be curious. Goblins consider it a virtue," he said, with only a hint of annoyance, "but it can lead to unfortunate occurrences."

Emmaline wondered what particularly he meant. She wished she had some way of gauging exactly how old he was, or where he really came from. She looked out to the west, but all she could see was more forest, and beyond that, the Wastes. She knew that far beyond this was the ocean and some islands. Could that have been where he'd come from?

"I suppose if I hadn't followed the tail of the goblin who cursed me, I wouldn't be a rabbit now," Emmaline said, not giving up on her plan just yet.

"Oh, yes," Sebastian said. "I haven't heard much about that. All Bostwick has told me was that you used to be a human. So goblins cursed you as well?"

"Yes. I'll never forget him. His horrible grinning face was the last thing I saw before I changed," she said, though it came out more bitterly than she expected. "What about you?"

Sebastian looked out the window before him, and when he spoke, it was with much sadness.

"I saw the Styx goblins: a crowd of colorful, vacuous fools, a disgrace to all the noble ideas held about them. All at once, there was a glowing cage around me, and I tried to escape, but couldn't. I couldn't stop them, even with my power, and then… it happened. I felt like every particle within me was on fire. I looked for help, and the only person who could have stopped it looked away. That was the last thing I saw with my true eyes."

"A human," Emmaline whispered. "Was the person who could have stopped it a human?"

"Yes. But I don't begrudge him for it, after what…Well, it doesn't matter. Ultimately, the Styx goblins are responsible for everything. After they trapped me into this wretched form, they chained me in the dungeon to rot."

"But surely they fed you?"

"Not a scrap. But don't worry," he said hastily, and began licking his paw, speaking between licks, "I caught mice."

"How long were you down there?" Emmaline said, feeling that finally they were getting somewhere.

"I'm afraid I don't know for sure. All I know is that Delilah found me one day and freed me, though my time in her company was perhaps worse than in the dungeon. She used to paw at me and pull my tail, acting like I was her personal plaything, put specifically on earth to amuse her. I have to say, she is the epitome of everything that is wrong with Styx."

"Well, she was just a child. Lots of children treat animals that way."

"But I'm not an animal," he said bitterly. "and she was *forty-seven*."

"Ohh…" Emmaline said, wondering what that would be in human years, but sure it was far too old to be considered a child.

"That's why I'm certain she would never help me. I suppose Bostwick told you of my request for the Domino?"

Emmaline nodded. "I guess we aren't so different after all."

"No… We're nothing alike. And you should be thankful for that."

"Shouldn't we wait for Emmaline?" Bostwick asked, as Millicent handed out bowls of bat-mushroom stew.

For several days now, Delilah had insisted that he and Emmaline eat dinner with Millicent and herself, instead of in Bostwick's room as they usually did. He sat a seat away from Delilah, who was at the head of an absurdly long table in the ballroom. The room itself could only be described as magnificent, with a tall ceiling from which chandeliers in the shapes of bat wings and spider webs hung. Two whole walls of the hexagonal room were taken up by windows looking out onto the night, while the other four had tall black and brown trees painted on them, no doubt to resemble the Forest of Infinite Horrors.

"She's on a secret mission," Delilah purred, as Millicent sat down between them. "Don't worry, we'll save some for her. If you don't eat it all first, of course."

"I won't," Bostwick said, putting down his spoonful of stew uneaten. "I was just really hungry that time. That was all."

The first time Millicent had prepared the stew, he'd expected it to be revoltingly musty. To his surprise, it was savory and delicious, and he'd eaten three bowls without even noticing. This time, when he'd accompanied Millicent to the town, he'd found that Delilah's shopping list called for three times as many ingredients.

"Now, now, there's no shame in the appreciation of good food. Eat as much as you like."

Bostwick was about to do so, but the queen continued staring in his direction, as if waiting for him to take a bite. As he raised the spoon to his mouth, her eyes widened in anticipation.

"Stop that!"

"Stop what?"

"Stop staring at me. I don't like people watching me when I eat."

The queen scoffed. "What a strange complex."

"It's not a complex! You keep looking at me like you're waiting for something to happen. It's creepy."

"I just want to see your look of joy when you eat the first spoonful. Is that so much to ask?"

"Yes," he said, and conjured a hanging curtain in front of Delilah's face. The queen erupted in laughter, pushing the curtain out of the way.

"How come Millie gets to watch you eat, hmm?"

"Because she isn't staring at me freakishly."

"Like this?" Delilah raised both eyebrows and batted her eyes manically.

Both women collapsed into giggles at this. Bostwick turned his chair away from them and finally began to eat his stew. He continued eating, though Delilah was being suspiciously quiet.

"Are you enjoying your stew?" she said after a while.

"Yes."

"Do you like *bat* meat?"

"Yes."

"Oh really?"

"Ye-aggh!" he screamed.

He turned around to see a giant pink bat sitting in Delilah's seat, resting its head in its thumb. Millicent was holding her mouth, trying desperately not to laugh. Delilah returned to her regular form as Bostwick walked out of the room, leaving his stew unfinished.

"Why does she do things like that?" he asked Millicent as they washed dishes afterward.

"You have to admit, it was funny."

"It was inane. She has one of the most powerful magical items in existence and she uses it for things like that. I doubt it was meant for such ridiculous purposes."

"You never know with goblins."

"That's true. They aren't exactly interested in practicality."

"They invented a way to grow pineapples underground," Millicent said in the goblins' defense.

"Really?"

"Over there," she said, pointing a pruny finger down one of the tunnels leading away from the kitchen, "is where all the pineapples in Styx grow, because the climate isn't right for them above ground."

"How does it work?" Bostwick asked, forgetting Delilah's nonsense for a moment.

"The pineapple chambers are under the garden. All the stepping stones and garden paths collect sunlight, and send it underground to the pineapple chamber. The stones are actually connected to these glowing flowers that grow on the ceiling and give the pineapples light and warmth."

"Like that one empty room in the castle?" Bostwick asked, remembering the upside-down plants.

"Yep. The Styx goblins bred them specifically for growing pineapples."

"The Academy uses something similar," Bostwick said. "Instead of making a flame, they somehow came up with a way to make something similar to sunlight itself, and send that through the entire academy. I wonder if it works the same way."

"Probably," Millicent said.

"I guess goblins can be pretty clever when it comes to magic. Still, I wish they were a little less adept at things like curses."

Millicent nodded and fell silent, thinking.

She was glad Bostwick was here, not just to teach her magic or help her clean, but just here beside her. She wished it could stay like this, but knew it couldn't. Eventually, she would have to convince Delilah to let Bostwick go, and Delilah would agree, and Bostwick would be only too glad to leave. He seemed happier in the recent weeks, though, when he could do more magic than cleaning. Even now as he was drying dishes, he had a placid expression that could almost pass for a smile.

"Bostwick, do you still hate it in Styx?"

He looked at her as if he'd awoken from a dream and blinked several times before answering.

"When I think of the entire situation, I want to scream," he said, as Millicent expected. "But it's better than traveling around the Ataxian wilderness. I get to sleep in an actual bed instead of on the ground, and instead of catching, conjuring, or buying food, most of which is semi-inedible to humans, I get to eat your cooking, which is just as good as the food in Camellia. And even though I'm not technically Delilah's court magician, I get to practice magic with you."

"But you'd still rather go, if you could? If you wouldn't get cursed?"

He paused again, as if trying to decide something.

"Of course I would. And yet, moment by moment, I don't mind it here so much. When I'm around Delilah, I feel like a bird in a cage, but when it's just Emmaline, Sebastian, and you, I barely remember that I'm in Styx. During magic lessons, or sometimes when we're cleaning, I'm even happy. It feels like I've always been doing this, like this is what I'm meant for. Almost the way it was when I began learning magic. Things were hard then too, but I knew that everything would be all right in the end. I know that I'll escape someday."

Seeing the sadness in Millicent's face, he hastily added, "But I'm not going to abandon you. If I leave Styx, you and Emmaline and Sebastian are coming with me. Whether it's cleaning or magic tricks or being held captive or being free, we're in this together. Even if it didn't start out that way, that's the way it is now."

Millicent looked into the soapy water pensively.

"Does that make sense?" Bostwick asked.

"Yes," she said finally. "It sounds sort of poetic, doesn't it?"

"Really?"

Millicent nodded, and Bostwick smiled self-consciously. They continued washing dishes in silence, side by side.

Ten

The Mad Bomber at Last

"Bostwiiick!" Delilah shrieked.

The queen glanced around the empty garden as if Bostwick would pop out from behind one of the bushes. When he did not appear, she tapped her foot several times, then proceeded to march into the castle. Eventually, she found him sitting in his room sipping iced tea through a straw and fanning himself with a book.

"Bostwick, why didn't you answer me," she said, sounding hurt. "I know you can hear me through the window.

"It's too hot outside today. Why? What do you want?"

"I was just going out to practice my croquet swing when I noticed that my toad lilies and cyclamen were all smashed to pieces. Why is that, Bostwick, hmm?"

"Millicent accidentally fell on them when we were practicing fire conjuration."

"She fell out the library window!" the queen gasped, grabbing Bostwick by the collar. "Good grief, man! What sort of magic have you been teaching her?"

"We were practicing outside," he said, removing her

hands. "It's too hot in the library."

"Too hot inside, too hot outside; make up your mind, Bostwick."

She made a grab for his tea—he presumed for some mischievous purpose—but he pulled it away from her just in time and continued sipping it. Defeated, Delilah sat in the chair opposite him and held her head in her hands.

"It has been getting a bit stuffy lately, but that's summer for you, eh? Still, that's no excuse for you to roll up your shirtsleeves. You're supposed to be a professional."

"You don't honestly expect me to work in this heat? Everyone in the Empire has the good sense to relax on days like this."

"Relax? Relax! *Bost*wick," she cried flamboyantly. "I know you've been in my family for generations, but any more of this nonsense and I'm afraid I'll have to let you go."

"Generations, huh?"

"I thought it sounded good at the time. Oh, teasing you isn't even fun in this heat, is it? I can't wait for monsoons to start, then maybe I'll force you to paint the castle or something."

Bostwick continued to sip his tea as the queen laid her chin on the table and looked up at him.

"You're not gonna react or anything?" Bostwick shook his head. "You're no fun. No one is any fun. I tried to get Emmaline to wear a carrot hat this morning, but she adamantly refused, and Millicent still doesn't want to wear the new dress I bought her. So much for being nice... Do *you* want to wear the new dress I bought her?"

"No."

"Didn't think so."

An insect flew past Delilah's face and her eyes followed it around the room. When it eventually landed on the table in front of her, she slammed her hand down on it, leaving nothing but a gooey black smear.

"Can you not kill bugs on my table?" Bostwick said. "I'd appreciate it."

"That's it!" she said, jumping up and spinning around with glee. "That's how we'll beat this heat. Black jelly!"

"What's...? Actually, never mind. I don't want to know."

"Black jelly," the queen explained, "is a goblin dessert made from a black grass that grows on the Gammon Coast. I was reminded because of the bug."

"I'm not eating anything that reminds you of bug innards."

"Oh, hush, Bostwick. It's a traditional summertime treat. I've been eating it ever since I first hatched from an egg."

"You... hatched from an egg?"

"Why?" she asked with glee. "Does that creep you out?"

"Yes."

"Fantastic! Anyways, you and Emmaline should go into town and get the jelly from Sticky Yum's Lolly Shop."

Bostwick cringed. He would infinitely prefer eating black bug jelly to whatever a sticky yum lolly was.

"And *you* can't get it because...?"

"Because I'm the queen and I have important dress-wearing propositions to discuss with Millicent. Just ask them for a big ol' bucket o' black jelly. They'll know what you mean."

"This is sounding less and less appetizing by the second."

♠ ♦ ♣ ♥ ♣ ♦ ♠

When Emmaline and Bostwick arrived in town, they found Sticky Yum's Lolly Shop immediately. It was not difficult to miss. The building closely resembled a wad of pink cotton candy, with a coating of an unidentified fluff clinging to the walls. Bostwick entered reluctantly to find the interior was covered in the same substance, and the proprietor of the shop, a goblin with enormous eyes and long, spidery arms, wore a hat made of it as well.

"Hello!" the creature cooed. "And what brings you to my shop this fine day?"

"I'm supposed to buy some black jelly," Bostwick said.

"Black jelly?"

"Yeah, black jelly. Delilah said it's a goblin treat that you sell."

"Black jelly?" it said again, scratching its head.

"I bet she did this on purpose," Bostwick said to Emmaline. "This place probably doesn't even sell sweets."

"'Course they sell sweets," someone behind Bostwick said. It was one of the Roly Police. "You just have to ask properly. How much black jelly did you want, then?"

"A bucket," Emmaline said.

"Hey, mister, these two'll have a scrumpcia-bucket of wigglicious black jelly, and I'll be havin' a box of easy-squeezy pineappular yum chunks, if you don't mind."

"Of course sir. Always happy to please a customer."

"Thank you for helping us," Emmaline said, as she, Bostwick, and the bugbear left the shop with their sweets.

"Don't mention it. That candy man is a particular sort of fellow. Care for a pineapple bit?" he said, offering the box to Bostwick.

"No thanks."

"You really should try them. I always get them in monsoon season."

"What's a monsoon?" Emmaline asked.

"Ah, you're a foreigner; I forgot. See those dark clouds over yonder?" He gestured to the eastern sky. "Those are big fat rain clouds. And when they get to Styx, monsoon season starts."

Bostwick was about to correct this simplistic explanation when five more bugbears rolled toward them and popped open. The big one and the mustachioed chief were among them.

"Good thing we caught up to you," the chief said. "Someone said they saw a goblin in a bomber jacket headed this way! That's got to be our suspect."

"A bomber jacket doesn't mean the person wearing it is a bomber," Bostwick said.

He was proven wrong immediately, as the sweet shop behind them exploded. A shockwave sent Bostwick face forward to the ground, almost crushing the tub-like container of jelly in his arms. The big bugbear dragged him and Emmaline behind a building across the narrow street. They peered out, but all they could see was a cloud of smoke and dust where the shop had once been. The candy man crawled out of it and wiped his face with a pink handkerchief.

"Oh, my beautiful shop!" he wailed. "What has become of you?"

Something shot out of the smoke and the candy man flounced away with exaggerated sobs. The police huddled behind the building, waiting. As they stood there, the dark clouds moved closer to town and a heavy wind picked up, sweeping the smoke away to reveal a pink and gray pile of fluffy, singed debris.

On top of the pile, in what looked like a dramatic pose that he was much too small to pull off, stood a two-foot tall goblin. He had a doglike face that was mostly taken up by his giant grinning mouth. He was dressed in a leather hat with goggles, a black bomber jacket, and tiny combat boots, and in his hands, which looked like pig trotters, he held a wrench. He turned to admire the wreckage, revealing two uselessly small, bat-like wings.

"What is that?" Bostwick asked.

"A Gremlin," the large bugbear replied. "Gents, I think we have found our mad bomber."

"Of course!" the chief said. "Gremlins are famous for rickety, badly put-together machines. Why didn't I think of that earlier?"

"Yes," said Bostwick. "Why didn't you?"

The bugbear shrugged—at least Bostwick assumed it was a shrug—and walked out from behind the wall to face the Gremlin.

"I am Jape Escapade, chief of the Roly Police. I demand that you give yourself up!"

"Not on your life, bugbear," the Gremlin said in a scratchy, squeaky voice. "I'm not going down without a fight.

In fact, I'm not going down at all!"

"At least identify yourself."

"I'm Balder D. Spleenbeck, Gremlin genius. But you can just call me 'Sir', or if you're feeling bold, 'Master' would work just as well."

"I've heard of you, Spleenbeck. The D stands for 'Dot', doesn't it?"

At this, Balder threw down his wrench and jumped up and down in a small circle.

"It's Dash!" he screeched. "Dash! Dash! Dash!"

"Balder Dash?" Bostwick said sarcastically. "Of course it is. What's he getting so worked up about?"

"Well, Dot is a pretty effeminate name," the big bugbear said. "I've heard of this guy before. A while back, he hung around Rigmarole, stealing famous artifacts, robbing banks, and holding a goat hostage for over a week before barbecuing and eating it. Mostly just flashy crimes done to make a name for himself. He's a raging egomaniac with an inferiority complex a mile wide. Not a good combination."

"Calm down, Spleenbeck," the chief called. "We just want to talk to you. What do you want?"

"Eh? Want?"

"What are your demands?"

"I demand that Styx be blown to itty bitty pieces, and that none of you stop me."

He pulled out what resembled a tiny blunderbuss, pointed it at the chief, and fired. A net shot out and covered him as he rolled into a sphere.

"The chief's down!" the big bugbear said. "Get the perp!"

The police rolled out, popping open just in time to see

Spleenbeck slide down the pile of rubble and run off.

"He's heading for the market!"

The big bugbear rolled after Spleenbeck, while the rest went in another direction to head him off. Bostwick and Emmaline were left alone amongst the debris.

"Should we go after them?" Bostwick asked.

"Of course! We may be able to help somehow. You can use your magic."

"Magic isn't exactly useful in combat situations," Bostwick said, "but I suppose it's worth a try.

They followed the large bugbear to the opening of the square that housed the kiosks and stalls that made up the market. Goblins of all shapes and sizes were already fleeing the scene, as stalls went up in flames behind them and produce rolled out into the street. The smell of smoke and gunpowder hung heavy in the air.

"I thought this guy's bombs never worked," Bostwick said, stopping beside the bugbear.

"If you make enough bombs, one of them's bound to work eventually. Chaos knows, he's had plenty of practice at it. Now, you two civilians stay here. I'm going to go in after him. Take cover. This could get messy."

Bostwick and Emmaline watched as he rolled away into the market, which was now in a state of pandemonium. He would stop behind overturned carts and the remains of food stalls to check his surroundings, but they soon lost sight of him as he was swallowed up in the crowd of fleeing goblins. They heard another explosion from the far side of the market and saw a cloud of smoke and dust rise into the air as another building went down.

"I can't believe one little goblin would cause so much trouble," Emmaline said. "No wonder the Empire didn't want them around. Shouldn't we do something?"

"I can't see a thing from here," Bostwick said, peering into the smoke. "Let's get a better look."

He entered the square and skirted his way towards the opposite side. He stopped suddenly when he saw the big bugbear lying face down on the ground.

"Is he dead?" Emmaline asked as Bostwick flipped him over to reveal a large bloody gash in his left side.

"No, he's breathing."

He set Emmaline and the tub of jelly down and pulled an up-ended crate over the bugbear's midsection to cast a healing spell.

"Will the spell work with a crate instead of a box?"

"I hope so, but it'll take a while, at any rate. I wish I could remember that incantation Millicent used."

"What about the other police, Bostwick? What if they're—"

She was cut off by a huge explosion behind them, as a row of kiosks went up in flames. From out of the fire walked the tiny silhouette of Balder Spleenbeck. As he came closer, they saw he was holding his blunderbuss in one hand and a bomb in the other.

"Well, well, well," he said, stopping five feet from them. "If I'd known I'd find a human here, I'd have brought a bigger bomb."

"Why are you doing this?" Emmaline asked, trying to give Bostwick more time to heal the bugbear.

"A talking rabbit? Not something you see everyday. I'll

answer your question, bunny. I'm doing this because I despise Styx, as all goblins should. Styxians are loathsome and vile, and the only thing worse than a Styx goblin is a human."

He pointed his gun at Bostwick, who was too busy casting his spell to defend himself. Emmaline launched herself at the Gremlin, knocking him back toward the row of burning kiosks. She began to bite him and scratch with her claws, but he shook her off, rolled to the side, and shot at her. This time, an actual bullet came out of his gun, narrowly missing her tail. He shot again, forcing her closer to the flames.

"Just what I need," he said, pressing a button on his bomb, "a rabid rabbit on my tail. Well, bunny, it looks like I'll be having hasenpfeffer tonight!"

He threw the bomb, which exploded a foot from Emmaline. The force of the explosion sent her flying. Balder watched her limp form fall back to earth with a look of delight on his face, which turned into a scowl when Bostwick caught her in his up-turned top hat.

"You're a magician?" he shrieked. "That's the very worst of the worst!"

Bostwick did not stick around to hear more. He ran back to where the big bugbear lay, healed but unconscious. Emmaline was alive, but had been knocked out by the bomb blast. Worst of all, some shrapnel had cut her side and her back leg. Bostwick knelt and quickly used another smaller crate to heal her, but in mid spell, he felt something being pressed against the back of his head.

"End of the line, human."

"You know," Bostwick said, more to buy time than

anything else, "even if you kill me, the Empire will come after you."

"Is that right?" Balder said, cocking his gun and pressing it harder into Bostwick's head.

"This rabbit you've injured is actually a human princess. You're not going to get away with this."

"So I'll take on the whole Empire. Big deal."

The spell was finished. Bostwick's mind raced with ideas, spells that could help in any way.

"Then I'll make myself the new Emperor," Balder continued, "as I've always fancied myself the royal type, and all you humans will be slaves. Not you, I suppose, as you'll be stone dead by then. Well, this is good-bye, and to think we only just met."

Bostwick spun and knocked the gun out of Spleenbeck's hands, then grabbed it—it was not much larger than a wine bottle—and threw it as far away as he could. Balder shrieked, threw a smoke bomb down, and made a run for it. Without thinking, Bostwick cast a levitation spell on one of the Gremlin's boots, sending the rest of him to the ground as he tried to take a step.

"Oh, the indignity," Balder said, tearing his floating boot off and shoving it away, "of a human using magic on me! I suppose you think you're special, do you? Just like a goblin eh? You don't know the meaning of the word 'magic'."

"And you do?"

"'Course I do. All goblins have their own speciality of magic; we Gremlins can summon objects from our home. And do you know what I've got at my home?"

Bostwick already knew what Balder was about to

summon, so he conjured up a curtain in mid air to act as a shield between him and the barrage of bombs being thrown in his direction. It only took three explosions before the curtain was in shreds, but by this time, Bostwick had run to the far side of the square, well out of range of the rest of the bombs.

"Running away like a weasel, are you? Try this one, then!"

Balder rolled a large metal ball out towards the magician. Bostwick dodged this easily, but the ball sprouted four spindly mechanical legs and changed course, scurrying in whatever direction he went. He pulled out a handkerchief, which he turned into a bird with the flick of his wrist, then released the bird into the air. It swooped past the bomb, which reared onto its back legs, stumbled, and turned over.

"Blast it all!" Balder shrieked as the bomb exploded yards away from Bostwick. He summoned another gun and fired before Bostwick could dodge. A strange ball of energy hit the magician and he fell to his knees, clenching his teeth. He was alive, but was entirely numb and couldn't move.

"You are infuriating," Balder said, tossing the gun into the air behind him, where it disappeared back to wherever his home was. "I was going to just shoot you in the back of the head, but you had to do all these magiciany tricks. Well, I'm not just going to kill you now. That would be too easy. I'm going to leave your fate up to this!"

He conjured a giant red bomb that was almost as big as he was with knobs and buttons sticking out all over it.

"We Gremlins call these beauties 'Death-Surprise'. See, no one can say what any one of them is capable of. Their innards are an everything-but-the-kitchen-sink stew of chemicals, combustibles, and machine parts. Sometimes they're duds, sometimes they wipe away whole villages. The only way to find out is to set it off!"

Bostwick desperately tried to move as Balder twisted the knobs and dials on the Death-Surprise. He felt some of the feeling coming back to his arms, and he could turn his head a bit.

"This'll explode on impact. Well, make a wish."

Balder threw the bomb into the air, his face taken up entirely by a delighted grin. Bostwick could feel his legs again, but knew that it was too late. The bomb seemed to fly through the air in slow motion, gliding up in a perfect arc. Bostwick somehow had time to think that his life would all be over in seconds. For some reason, he was very annoyed, because now he would never get to see Millicent pull a rabbit out of a hat. He even had time to wonder why that was his last thought, and why time seemed to slow down and stretch out so much before death. *Well*, he thought, *so much for my last thought*.

When the bomb reached its zenith, twenty feet in the air, Bostwick saw something out of the corner of his eye come spinning towards it. He thought it looked like a pink croquet mallet, but before he could tell, it slammed into the bomb.

Instantly, the air around the bomb was enveloped in a searing blue fireball. It burned for at least five seconds, disintegrating the bomb casing and the remains of a kiosk that had been caught in the blast. The blue light reflected eerily in Balder's goggles as he looked toward Bostwick, who was completely still, even as the fire dissipated. Only the very front of his hair was singed. The air between him and the

Gremlin still simmered as they both turned to look at the tall figure who had thrown the mallet.

"No one," Delilah said, "blows up my butler. Bostwick, take this!"

She flung something vaguely spear-shaped at him. He caught it, movement returning to him at last, but saw that it was nothing but a common household mop.

"Mop up the floor with him!"

"You've got to be kidding," Bostwick and Balder said in unison.

"It's your destiny! Von Dogsbody blood flows in your veins. You must accept that!"

"Accept this!" Balder cried, and drew his gun out once more. He fired another energy blast at Bostwick, who blocked it with the mop. The Gremlin fired again and again, but to no avail. He shoved his mouth to one side of his face and turned his gun on Delilah.

"Well, I suppose killing the Queen of Styx is just as good as killing a magician."

Delilah merely raised her eyebrows and looked unimpressed.

"And this time," Spleenbeck said, turning a dial on the gun, "I'll use full blast. May the world know, here and now that I, Balder Dash Spleenbeck, greatest of Gremlins—"

"Don't you mean Balder *Dot*?" Bostwick said.

Spleenbeck hurled his gun to the ground, where it broke into pieces, and screamed, "MY NAME IS DASH! Darn your eyes with knitting needles! I'll destroy every last one of you! Say hello to your doom!"

He pulled out of the air behind him, not a bomb, but a

small clock. He looked just as surprised as Bostwick was, and threw the clock behind him. He tried to summon a bomb again, but pulled out a teakettle. Next came a chair, a bar of soap, and jar of pickles. By now his tiny pig hands were shaking, and his large mouth had begun to quiver.

"Let me guess," Delilah said. "You were a little too exuberant with your destruction of my market, and now you're all out of bombs."

Balder paused briefly, then spun around to make a run for it, but crashed into the large bugbear, who was awake and angry. He picked the struggling Gremlin up in one hand and walked up to Delilah.

"Well, case closed, I suppose. What do you want us to do with him?"

"I'll kill you in your sleep!" Balder squeaked.

"Take him up to the castle. There's a nice clean dungeon cell waiting for him."

"But first," Balder continued, "I'll wake you up so you can feel it. I'll wait till you get married and have children, just so I can orphan them, and then I'll—"

"You know what your problem is?" Delilah said. "You have much too big of a mouth."

He tried to bite her hand, but the bugbear had already begun heading toward the castle. A few of the other police bugs, including the chief, started to emerge from the wreckage, though most were in much worse condition than the big one. One even had a large dent in his shell.

"Heal them up, please, Bostwick."

Bostwick did so, emptying a box full of turnips for the job.

"It's a good thing you showed up when you did," he admitted, after he had healed the third bugbear to come to him. "But how did you know the bomber would be here?"

"The columns of black smoke rising to the heavens, and the screams of the townsfolk kind of clued me in."

"Oh."

"I'm glad you managed to hold him off until I came. We make a good team, hmm?"

Bostwick said nothing until Delilah poked him in the shoulder several times.

"Maybe you should work on putting the fires out," he said.

"Hmph. Suit yourself."

"All of that happened while I was knocked out?" Emmaline asked.

They were sitting in the greenhouse of the castle, watching the rain and lightning out the window while Delilah and Bostwick recounted the day's events. Bostwick was forced to correct Delilah's many embellishments.

"I wish I could have been more help."

"Nonsense, Emmaline. You protected the black jelly, and that's what's important."

"What about the market?" Millicent asked. "What are all those merchants going to do now?"

"The police are taking care of everything. Really, I should give them all a raise after this. Hopefully there will be no more Balder Spleenbeck-types running around."

"So he was trying to blow up the map of Styx to destroy

the whole country?" Sebastian asked.

Millicent stared pointedly at Delilah, who rolled her eyes and sighed.

"Oh, that's right, you *weren't* actually the mad bomber, so you wouldn't know. Well, when the first dozen bombs didn't work, he finally wised up and realized that I was the only one who could damage the map. So he decided to blow Styx up personally, bit by bit."

"But if he had destroyed the map while he was in Styx, wouldn't he have died, too?"

"He probably didn't consider that," Bostwick said. "He's not exactly what you would call stable."

"Well, he's safely locked away in the dungeon," said Delilah, who scooped heaps of black gelatin out into bowls and passed them around. "The police are taking care of the damages, and the monsoons have finally started. Now all that's left is to enjoy our black jelly."

Delilah took a heavy spoonful and closed her mouth around it. Bostwick, Millicent, and Emmaline tentatively followed suit, then grimaced in unison.

"Um, it's a little…" Millicent said, pushing her bowl away.

"It's better than I expected," Emmaline said politely.

Bostwick prodded the jelly with his spoon.

"It has absolutely no flavor whatsoever."

"Maybe you just have no taste," Delilah said, eating another spoonful.

Eleven

Thanks for the Memory

Millicent peered around the corner to make sure the hallway beyond was empty before hurrying down it. Her eyes shot from left to right, making sure no one was around to see her as she made her way around the castle, opening windows to let the cool monsoon air in. It was hard to be stealthy, however, because whenever she moved, her clothes made a loud rustling noise that was too loud to be dampened by the rain drumming against the roof.

She caught sight of herself against the window glass and shuddered.

The whole point of this outfit, Delilah had explained, was to be seen, but that was the last thing Millicent wanted. It was only because of Delilah's constant pestering notes and hints, which had culminated yesterday in a sleepless night of arguing and outright begging, that she had finally conceded to wearing the dress. But only today, and never again. Even now, she was sure she had only agreed to it due to lack of sleep.

When she reached the floor where Emmaline's and

Bostwick's bedrooms were, she held her skirt to keep the noise down and tip-toed down the hall, only to meet Emmaline as she was hopping out of her room. The rabbit stopped in her tracks and looked up in awe at Millicent.

"Well," said Emmaline after a moment, "don't you look different this morning?"

It was true. Millicent's new dress was as different from her usual straight and simple attire as a peacock was to a pigeon. She wore an intensely pink, lacy dress with giant puff sleeves and layers and layers of petticoats. Her apron was equally extravagant, with frills around the edges and large, heart shaped pockets. Around her neck was a pink, heart-shaped locket big enough to hold an entire family portrait. To complete the look, her hair was curled into ringlets and ordained with an enormous magenta bow that was larger than her head.

"Oh," said Millicent, blushing. "Delilah got me this dress, and she's been asking me to wear it, so I finally have."

"You don't look too happy about it, though."

"It's just so… embarrassing. I don't want anyone to see me like this."

"It's all right," Emmaline said, trying to assuage Millicent's worries. "It's only Bostwick and myself who'll see you. Besides, the dress isn't that, um… I mean, you look cute in it, even if it is a bit over the top."

Millicent looked downcast and doubtful. Emmaline decided to change the subject.

"So, let's get going on some of the morning's chores shall we? What's up for today?"

"Delilah wants Bostwick to fix the leaks in the roof and

then clean the laboratory."

"Well, we better get to it, then," Emmaline said, and hopped to Bostwick's door.

"Oh, that's all right," Millicent said hastily. "He can do it later. We should let him sleep in."

"I'm sure he's awake already."

"Well, still, he needs his rest. He's probably still exhausted from that ordeal with the bomber."

"That happened a week ago. He's fine."

Emmaline knocked on his door with her paw as Millicent weighed whether she should run for it or simply hide in Emmaline's room. Before she could decide, the door opened. Bostwick stood in his doorway and stopped dead at the sight of Millicent.

"What is... *that?*" he asked.

"Oh," Millicent said, panicking, "this is a dress Delilah made me wear. She says it's the latest thing in the Empire, and although it's not exactly my taste in attire, Emmaline says it's cute. So, um, what do you think?"

Bostwick didn't say anything, but continued to stare at the dress. Slowly, his eyes traveled to the bow on her head, then to the two heart-shaped pockets, then to the outfit entire.

"So, do you like it?" she asked.

There was a beat of silence.

"No."

Millicent said nothing, but her face made it clear that she had never in her life heard a more distressing sound than Bostwick's answer. Emmaline pounced on Bostwick, sending him flat on his back into his room.

"How can you possibly say that to a girl?" she said, sitting on his chest and jabbing him with her front paws. "Can't you see she's embarrassed already as it is?"

"Well, who wouldn't be?"

"Stop that! Honestly, Bostwick, have you no ounce of human compassion? How would you feel if you had to wear something that didn't suit you?"

"'Didn't suit' doesn't really go far enough. 'Garish affront to the eyes' seems more appropriate. Don't blame me for telling the truth," he added, trying to avoid her accusing gaze, though she filled up most of his field of vision. "It's that psycho queen that made her wear it, not me."

"It doesn't matter who made anyone wear anything. The point is that when a girl asks your opinion of what she's wearing, you never, ever say, in a single, heartless syllable, that you don't like it. Especially not if that girl likes you."

"Huh?"

"Millicent. I think, call it rabbit's intuition if you like, but I get the feeling she may have a crush on you."

Bostwick was silent.

"Well, say something!"

"The door's open."

"What?"

"The door. She can hear everything we've been saying."

Emmaline froze in utter terror. She hopped to the door and peered out. Millicent was standing still as a statue and red as a tomato. She looked like she wanted nothing more than to cease existing altogether. That not being an option, she ran as fast as she could down the hallway, turned the corner and disappeared.

"Now what?" Bostwick asked, getting to his feet.

"Now you go find her and apologize."

"If memory serves correctly, you were the one that blurted out her secret and made her run away."

"*You* insulted her."

"I insulted the dress!" he gasped, affronted by Emmaline's allegation.

"It's the same thing!"

"No, it isn't. All I said—" He stopped, rehashing the conversation in his head for a few seconds, then grimaced in dawning comprehension.

"Well, either way," he mumbled, "she probably doesn't wants to see me right now."

"Well, you can bet she doesn't want to see me, and I refuse to allow her to be all alone at a time like this, so you better go find her. And furthermore, if you don't go, I'll ruin your every waking moment, I'll devour your top hat and I'll… I'll tell Delilah what you said!"

Although that was hitting below the belt, Bostwick didn't want to stick around and say so. He ran down the hallway and turned to follow where Millicent had gone. Finding her proved to be a remarkably easy task, as she was sobbing loudly from a broom closet at the far end of the hall. Bostwick was about to open the door, but thought better of it. Instead, he sat against the wall next to the door and cleared his throat to announce his presence. There was an immediate hush in Millicent's crying, as if a sudden silence would disguise the fact that she was there.

"It's me," said Bostwick.

Millicent did not respond, but gave a small, shuddering sob.

What was he supposed to say? That he liked her dress? He didn't. That Emmaline hadn't thought about what she was saying? That was obvious. Or should he say that he'd known all along that she had a crush on him and that he felt the same way about her? That simply wasn't true.

What he wished was to simply say something to let her know that he didn't want her to be sad or worry so much about everything he said. He, of course, never put very much store in anything really, and for the life of him couldn't see how she could care so much about him or what he thought. A part of him felt bad for not returning her affection, but another part didn't have feelings one way or the other. And, most mystifying to him, was the smallest part of him that really did care, that wanted to tell Millicent right out that he loved her and couldn't stand to see, or hear, her crying, that wanted nothing more than to sit with her, perfectly happy and smiling, at a picnic by the river under a tree. But that part was so small that he barely noticed it, for he was too busy trying to come up with some way of communicating all the complex and complicated things he felt. In the end, there was only one thing he could think to say.

"I'm sorry I hurt your feelings, Millicent."

And somehow, in the infinitely chaotic way that things have of happening in Styx, his message, in this one utterance, was understood entirely.

Millicent, still sniffling slightly, reached her hand under the door and held Bostwick's. He, not being as complete a cad as Emmaline made him out to be, let her hold it.

The two sat there like that for at least an hour, and when Bostwick eventually opened the door, he found that Millicent had fallen asleep. Carefully, and with the aid of a levitation spell, he carried her back to her room and laid her on the bed. He looked back at her only once, then closed the door with a small snap. He sighed and felt, for the briefest of moments, like going on a picnic.

As he left, a ladybug who had witnessed the whole affair flew off Bostwick's shoulder and crept under Millicent's door. The insect scurried across the floor and up to Millicent's bed, and in an instant transformed into the Queen of Styx. Reaching down, she unclasped the chain of Millicent's necklace and delicately placed the locket in a small jar she was carrying. She then spun on her heel and walked to the door.

"Millie, hey, wake up!," she called loudly.

Millicent's eyes opened blearily. They were still red from crying.

"You overslept. But you still look tired, and maybe a little ill. How do you feel?" Delilah asked, coming over to the bed and holding her wrist up to Millicent's forehead. "No temperature; that's good."

"What time is it? Oh my, did I fall asleep wearing this? It's all wrinkled! Delilah, I'm sorry, I—"

"Never mind that," she said, holding a finger up to Millicent's lips. "In fact, I've changed my mind about the whole thing! You don't need to wear the dress after all."

"But—"

"Nope. Nothing you can say will change my mind. Anyway, after you get changed, come see me in the throne room, okay?"

"Uh, okay."

Delilah spun and left the same way Bostwick had. As she walked down the hall to the throne room, she looked at the jar in her hand.

"Hmm," she said to herself, "I do believe this will all work out nicely." Then she chuckled in her low, mysterious way, and continued on in silence.

"What are you going to say, Bostwick?" Emmaline asked. "It's not as if she can undo what's been done. I think if you give it a little time, everything between you and Millicent will go back to normal."

"First off, there is nothing between us, and second, this is about more than today's incident. I've had it with Delilah acting like she can just tell people to do whatever she wants."

"I agree, but I doubt that she'll really listen. She's pretty headstrong, you know?"

"Well, so am I, and I'm sick of not saying anything."

Emmaline sighed, but stayed silent. Bostwick threw open the doors to the throne room and marched in, Emmaline hopping after him. Lightning flashed, throwing the throne into silhouette, and rain pounded against the stained glass clock. The queen lay lazily across the seat and gazed at Bostwick serenely as he approached the stone steps.

"Hello, Bostwick."

"What is wrong with you?" he demanded.

"You know, I honestly wasn't expecting you to ask me that. I don't even have a sarcastic answer."

"What exactly were you trying to pull, making Millicent

wear that ridiculous get-up?"

"You really want to know?"

"Yeah. That's why I asked."

"I was hoping you would be enchanted by her beauty and finally realize your feelings of love for her that you have secretly had all along."

Bostwick opened his mouth but stopped before saying anything.

"Are... are you serious?" Emmaline asked.

"Of course I am! Don't you trust me?"

"I don't trust you as far as I can throw you," Bostwick replied, "which unfortunately, isn't far."

"Touché," Delilah said. "But I assure you, I'm telling the truth."

"Well, it doesn't matter, because your bizarre little scheme didn't work."

"That's just because you have no taste in clothing."

"Those clothes were hideous! Why would you make her wear something you knew she'd hate?"

"I—"

"Oh, I'm not done yet. First, you treat her like some kind of doll you can dress up, then expect that to magically make me like her?"

"You don't like her?" Delilah said, looking shocked.

"Not like that I don't. And then Emmaline blurted out that Millicent likes me, which I'm sure you intended to have happen sooner or later, and Millicent found out and, and..."

"And?" she asked, raising an eyebrow.

"And now everything is going to be awkward between us. We still have to work together, in close proximity. I'll be surprised if she can look me in the eye ever again."

"So?"

"So you messed everything up because you're always manipulating people. What are we to you, anyway? Just pawns in some game?"

"Oh, Bostwick. I had hoped that after all this time, you could come to think of us as friends," Delilah said with a wide smile.

"And I suppose Millicent's your friend? Is that why you dress her up and put her in weird situations to humiliate her?"

"You were the one who made her cry." Her voice had lost all the joviality it had a moment ago. Though her face was placid, her yellow eyes glared furiously from behind the Domino.

"How did you know that?" Emmaline asked. "Bostwick never said she cried."

Delilah smirked.

"I know what goes on in my own castle."

"So you were watching the whole time?" Bostwick asked. "Found it pretty amusing, did you? A live human romance playing out just for you? You have got to be the most—"

But before he could finish, the throne room door creaked open. Millicent came in, wearing a plain yellow dress and white apron. She slowly walked up to the throne and stopped a few feet from where Bostwick stood. She looked from him to Delilah and said nothing.

"Um, hi, Millicent," Bostwick said, already cringing from the awkwardness of the situation.

"Hi," she said with a little smile. "Delilah, you wanted something?"

"Yes, yes! I was wondering if you might prepare a light brunch for us."

"Of course! What would you all like?"

"A peanut butter and black jelly sandwich would be just lovely. And what will you have, Emmaline?"

"I... uh, I'll just have a small salad," she said unsurely.

"All right," said Millicent. "What about you, Bostwick?"

Bostwick looked blankly at Millicent, then at Delilah, then back to Millicent.

"I'm not hungry."

"Are you sure? It's no trouble."

"I'm fine."

"Okay," she said, and walked to one of the many doors in the wall that led to the kitchen.

Bostwick waited until she shut the door before addressing Delilah.

"What did you do?"

"Hmm? Whatever are you talking about?"

"She's acting like nothing happened!"

"Hmm..."

"You did something to her! I know you did!"

"Hmm, maybe I did. But can you figure out what?" She took out Millicent's locket and spun it around by the chain.

"Where did you get that?"

"From Millie. That was too easy. Ask something else."

"I'm not playing a guessing game! Tell me what you did!"

"What you should have asked," Delilah continued, ignoring Bostwick's protest, "is what was *in* the locket? I'll give you a hint: something close to Millie's heart, but closer to her mind."

"Delilah!"

"Fine, if you won't ask a question, then I'll do it." She sat up straight in her seat and pulled out a small jar which contained a white satchel. "Do you know how to make a memory?"

Neither Bostwick nor Emmaline said anything.

"Well?"

"You took her memory," Emmaline said, comprehending exactly what that satchel meant.

"You guessed it! Well, you had a bit of help, but still, congratulations."

"Wait," said Bostwick. "By 'took her memory,' you mean she doesn't remember anything?"

"Nothing that happened from the time she put on the lovely pink dress to the time I removed this necklace. Not one thing. Lucky thing, too. See, I figured you might be stupid enough to not be instantly wooed by Millie's dressed up form, and I assumed that would mean a disaster would ensue, so I put this memory collecting satchel in the locket just in case. Clever, eh?"

"You're insane!"

"That's two for two, Bostwick. Again, I have no witty comeback."

"You can't go around stealing people's memories!"

"It's better this way, Bostwick. Things will be normal between you and her, like you wanted, and Millie won't have to endure the memory of such an awful experience. She's so sweet and timid, I don't think she could bear it."

"Delilah, you can't possibly think that justifies taking something as important as her memory," Emmaline said.

"Of course I do. But that's not all. Bostwick still remembers what happened. I think it's a bit of a learning experience."

"How—"

"Oh," she smirked, "I'm not done yet. Hmm… You see, Bostwick, you tend to shoot your mouth off without thinking. I believe your exact response to Millie's question about her dress was 'No', which caused Emmaline to become so irate that, amidst her various admonitions of your conduct, she let slip Millie's secret. Don't worry, Emmaline, I don't blame you."

"So it's all my fault?" Bostwick asked furiously.

"Yes. But don't worry. I actually think you handled it rather well." Again the queen's expression changed, this time becoming softer, almost friendly. "We all say careless things sometimes, but you went after her, and that's what's important. So, as it turns out, you've learned, I hope, to watch what you say, and with my memory scheme, Millie is no worse for wear. Everything is good, see?"

Emmaline and Bostwick stood in silence, one stunned and the other fuming.

"Well, you'll both understand later. Now, I don't know about you, but I'm famished."

She stood up and walked past them, stopping only when she came to the throne room door.

"Coming?"

"We'll eat later," Bostwick said, through gritted teeth.

"But Emmaline ordered a salad."

"I'll be fine," Emmaline said.

"Suit yourself," said the queen, who continued out

through the door.

Bostwick picked Emmaline up without a word and walked to the door that led upstairs.

"Where are we going, Bostwick?"

"To see Sebastian."

"But, Bostwick…"

"I know you don't trust him, but whatever he is, he can't be worse than Delilah."

Sebastian was wandering around the treasure chamber as he so often did. He was examining a finely embroidered blue and white military coat so thoroughly that he didn't hear Bostwick approach.

"Sebastian. I'll get the Domino for you, but I'll need your help."

"What?" Emmaline said before Sebastian could respond. "Bostwick, I know what Delilah's done seems…"

"Diabolical."

"It doesn't matter. You can't do something so drastic," she said, glancing sideways at Sebastian. "Even if you get the Domino, Delilah can still curse you for deserting her."

"It doesn't matter. You and Millicent need to get away from her. We're nothing but pawns to her. Who knows what she'll do when she gets tired of us?"

"So you're all right with being cursed?"

"Yes, all right! I don't care if she curses me!" he yelled, but he looked nervous. After composing himself, he said stiffly, "Look, I'm still your court magician, so it's up to me to make sure you're safe, even if that means getting cursed."

"And Millicent?"

"What about her?"

"You seem to be very concerned about her."

Bostwick sighed.

"She deserves better than this, Emmaline. I don't know why she's working here, or why she thinks Delilah is her friend, but I can't just leave her to be toyed with and enslaved. You both need to escape. Don't worry about me."

"That's noble of you," Sebastian said at last. "What's gotten you into such a serious mood?"

"Delilah stole Millicent's memory," Emmaline said.

There was no need to explain further. Sebastian's ears shot back flat against his head and a low hiss came from his throat, sounding more cat-like than anything else he'd ever said.

"What kind of fool would tell her how to steal memories?" he asked lividly, then paced around the room. "Bostwick is absolutely right. We've got to go through with my plan at once."

"What plan?"

"A plan that will ensure that all three of you are free from Delilah's clutches, and that, hopefully, will not result in Bostwick being cursed."

"So what does this plan involve?" Emmaline asked suspiciously. Sebastian flicked his tail and wound around the legs of the glass suit of armor.

"That little Gremlin gave me an idea. Why don't we get a hold of the map of Styx, and hold it hostage in exchange for your freedom?"

"That's no good," Bostwick said. "She knows we can't harm the map, and it'll only make her angrier."

"There's more to my plan than only that," he said

mysteriously, "but that part will only come once I have my true form back. For now, why don't you focus on retrieving the Domino from Delilah?"

"Right," Bostwick said, already imagining what curse the queen would bestow on him for a second attempt at stealing her mask.

"When you have it, bring it to your room and hide it well. We must make sure Delilah knows nothing. I'll meet you there when you've got it," Sebastian said, and left through the window.

"There's something he isn't telling us," said Emmaline. "I think he's much more dangerous than Delilah. She's kept things from us, I know, but it's almost like a game to her. Sebastian is deliberately hiding something."

"And yet it's Delilah's games that end up getting us injured or almost eaten by wyrms or humiliated. Swear that you won't tell her what we're planning."

"What?"

"No matter what Sebastian does or how suspicious he seems, you can't tell anything to Delilah. It could ruin everything."

Emmaline glared at him angrily, and he stared pleadingly back.

"Very well. I promise I will not tell Delilah that you're attempting to steal her Domino or that Sebastian is planning to help us escape. Satisfied?"

Bostwick nodded and Emmaline hopped away. She'd left herself enough room for loop holes in her promise. Now, she just hoped she wouldn't have to go to Delilah for help.

Twelve

Sebastian's Transformation

Delilah continued to act as if nothing had happened three days before. She still heckled Bostwick as he went about his daily chores and made him do inane tasks alongside Millicent, who still trusted Delilah completely. Bostwick and Emmaline had decided not to tell her what had happened, in part because she would most likely not believe them, and partly because Bostwick did not want to do anything to upset Delilah as he worked out a way to get the Domino.

"You could suggest she throw another sleepover," he told Emmaline as he dusted the picture frames in the Hall of Portraits, "and then leave when she gives you the Domino."

"Because that won't look suspicious at all," Emmaline said.

"We could wait till she's asleep again, and then switch it with another mask."

"We don't have another mask, and I can't imagine that costume accessories would be in high demand in Ataxia. Even if they were, we can't buy one in town until all the shops are rebuilt."

"What about some place off the beaten path?" Bostwick

said. "Do you think, maybe, they have a mask at Rare and Priceless Counterfeits?"

"Of course I have a fake Domino of Nonpareil. What do you take me for?" Polkory said as she chiseled away at a block of marble.

"Can I see it?" Bostwick asked.

"It's over in that pile of clothes," she replied without turning around.

Bostwick sorted through the greatcoats, stockings, and mismatched boots until he found a plain black mask that looked indistinguishable from Delilah's.

"What does it do?"

"Put it on and find out."

Bostwick pulled out a pouch full of coins. Delilah had given it to him after Spleenbeck's attack as "bonus pay."

"I would prefer not to. How much does it cost?"

"Depends on what you want it for."

"It's for Delilah."

"Oh. Well, in that case, ten standard pin-a-pleys should do, and that's a bargain. Give it here," she said when Bostwick opened the coin purse and looked in questioningly. She removed ten of the medium sized coins and handed the purse back to him.

"Send the queen my regards," she called as he left the shop.

"Do you think Bostwick's been acting a little strange?" Millicent asked.

Delilah sipped her tea carefully before answering. She was lounging upside-down on the ceiling of glowing flowers while Millicent sat perched at the top of a ladder, balancing a tea tray in her lap. Below them, a field of pineapple plants reflected the yellow light from above.

"Well, he did volunteer to go grocery shopping all on his own today. Maybe he wants to try his hand at cooking."

"I don't think that's it," Millicent said. "He's been a lot quieter lately. And I've noticed that he seems really angry whenever you're around."

"Hmm."

Delilah steadied her cup, which was threatening to spill over. Though she had practiced upside-down tea drinking all her life, it was still a bit of an ordeal. Millicent sipped her own tea, but looked up at Delilah from the rim of her cup.

"I'm not going to let him go, Millie. I can tell that's what you're thinking, but it simply won't happen. I've told you before, I'm determined to make him fall for you."

"And I've told you that you can't *make* something like that happen. I hate thinking that Bostwick is trapped here because of some misguided matchmaking scheme."

"Well, it's not *just* that. What about my feelings, hmm?"

"You mean punishing him for stealing the Domino?"

"Nothing of the kind. I've just been thinking, lately, that before Bostwick came, I would have let him go in a heartbeat. I might very well have thrown him out myself. But now, well, I like him too much to let him leave. Does that make sense?"

Millicent nodded, but looked serious.

"I'd be sad if he wasn't here, Millie."

"You'd still have me."

A trickle of tea spilled downward from Delilah's cup. She righted the cup and stared up at the flowers around her.

"Of course I would," she said loftily, "but you'd be sad without him, too. Plus, you aren't done learning magic yet."

"That's true, but President Wilfrock sent me here to learn from *you*, not Bostwick."

"True, true, but I think it's clear from how little you've learned under my tutelage that I'm simply no good as a teacher."

"That's only because I always get sidetracked cleaning and you have to deal with bombers and pineapples and things."

"No, Bostwick is much better for you, Millie. That's why he should stay here with you."

Millicent sipped her tea thoughtfully for a moment, then finally said, "Then how about this: as soon as Bostwick has taught me everything about magic, he can leave if he wants. He'd certainly have worked hard enough to make up for stealing the Domino by then, especially," she added pointedly, "since he never got away with stealing it in the first place."

Delilah sat perfectly still, then threw her cup across the ceiling. As it shattered somewhere amongst the pineapples, she twirled in the air and hovered next to Millicent, an impish grin on her face.

"That sounds fair. But it must be all the magic that you would normally learn in the Academy. I think that's a lovely idea!"

"I wish you wouldn't throw so many dishes," Millicent

chided, though she was beaming. "Can we tell Bostwick?"

"Heck, no!" Delilah said, becoming serious. "We'll let him stew. You'll at least allow me that little pleasure."

Bostwick waited until midnight, then crept up to Delilah's room alone, with only a tiny flame spell for light. When he reached the top of the spiral staircase, he extinguished the spell and crept into the room. It looked just as it had months ago, when he first attempted to steal the Domino. Delilah lay sideways across her bed, tangled in her sheets, with her eyes closed.

"Delilah?" Bostwick said, "Can you hear me?"

"Pat them on the head," she mumbled, "and make casual conversation with them."

Satisfied that she was thoroughly unconscious, he took the Domino from her face and replaced it with the fake. He tucked the real mask under his coat and left the room, careful to avoid the vase that blocked his path.

The next morning, he and Emmaline waited in his room for Sebastian.

"This is your last chance to turn back, Bostwick," Emmaline said. "We can just tell Sebastian we couldn't get the Domino. Or say we've changed our minds about escaping."

"Don't trust me?" the cat asked, jumping into the room from the window. "I very much doubt that you've changed your minds. Do you have the Domino, Bostwick?"

Bostwick held out the mask for the cat to see. Emmaline looked disapprovingly at it.

"How does it work?" Sebastian asked.

"Just will yourself to look like your true form and that should do the trick."

"It's been a long time, but I remember."

Bostwick held the mask to Sebastian's face and waited. He and Emmaline took a collective breath.

In a blur of black and white, Sebastian changed, shedding his feline form and growing taller and taller, finally stopping when he was about the same height as Delilah. Emmaline gazed at him in shock. She had seen him before—his long pointed ears, delicate features, and narrow shoulders—had walked past his image dozens of times without thinking, every time she went down the hall of portraits. There were slight differences, true, for his hair, running down his back in a long braid, was white, not sea green, and his eyes had human irises, though they were yellow as they had been in the painting. The goblin in the pictures had been dressed in ornate robes; Sebastian wore a tunic and pants that looked eerily similar to the Academy's uniform. His face, which was bluish white in color, was not grinning carefreely now, but was difficult to read as he stared down at his hands. He looked relieved and tired and depressed, his new face so much more expressive than a cat's.

Emmaline hopped back, afraid. He was the man from the portrait; he had to be, even though that picture was nearly three hundred years old. Perhaps he looked different due to the passage of time. It was said immortal beasts were shape changers; perhaps this was what they meant.

Bostwick looked like he wanted to say something, but words failed him. He simply stared at Sebastian, who stared down at himself. He turned his arms over, examining blue-black piebald markings that ran up his forearms, then tentatively felt his face with his long, thin fingers. He seemed to shrink inward as he felt the skin and bones of his face, like it was too much for him. Emmaline wondered how long had it been since he'd been able to feel skin instead of fur.

At last, he took a long breath and looked at them with a small, weary smile.

"Thank you, Bostwick. Now, shall we get back to the matter at hand?"

Bostwick blinked as if waking from a trance.

"Of course. What do you need?"

Sebastian paused to think and looked quite statuesque. After a moment, he turned without a word and started walking out of the room, as if sure they would follow. They did.

"As of now you two should start preparing to leave, in a hurry if we must. Pack everything, and tell Millicent to do the same."

"She won't listen. She doesn't understand what Delilah's been doing to her," Bostwick said.

Sebastian stopped, looking unsure for the first time.

"Pack *for* her if you must," he said. "Take anything you believe is valuable to her. You should be ready by noon. Meet me in the treasure chamber. I'll tell you the rest of my plan then."

Bostwick ran to do as commanded, leaving Emmaline alone with Sebastian.

"What about you?" she asked. "Where will you be until then?"

"I will retrieve the map of Styx," he said simply, and strode away down the next hall.

Emmaline froze as everything in her mind fit together like puzzle pieces. She felt like she was sinking through the floor, and cursed her small rabbit feet as she hopped frantically to find Delilah.

Instead, she found Millicent in the greenhouse, watering plants.

"Where's Delilah?" she asked urgently.

"She went to town to see how the rebuilding of the market is going. Is everything all right, Emmaline? You're shaking."

"I don't have time to explain. I have to talk to her right away. Can you take me? We have to use the automobile; it's the fastest way."

"Let's go!"

Millicent smiled, delighted at the prospect of driving. Emmaline would have explained her theory on the way, but she didn't want the maid to worry about the danger that all of them were in.

Thirteen

Free to Go

Emmaline and Millicent (who was not a half bad automobile driver) arrived in the town to find what looked like the entire population of Styx out working to rebuild the market. Millicent parked the car in a side street and stood on the hood to see over the heads of the many goblins who were running back and forth with supplies. She finally spotted Delilah's pink hair amongst all the fur, feathers, and scales, and waded through the sea of goblins with Emmaline held high above her head to guide the way.

When they made it to Delilah, they saw that she was conversing with Heather, who was looking extremely put out.

"They're getting it all wrong," the mapmaker said, pointing to a piece of paper she held in her hand. "That building is supposed to go under this sauce stain, here."

"I think it fits much better on top of the mushroom stall," Delilah said, looking mischievously delighted.

"It'll fall right over! Hey, Greeny," Heather called, addressing Millicent, "look at that building. Does that look structurally sound to you?"

Millicent looked at the building Heather indicated, which

nested precariously on a bundle of long sticks that threatened to give way at the next breeze. Under this were the burnt remains of the mushroom stall.

"Um, not really."

"There, you see?" Heather said, as if the matter was settled.

"But Shenanigan said she wanted her store up there," the queen said.

"Well, I'm the one who drew the map, so I say where her store goes, unless she'd like it better if she sold shoe soles up in the Wastes, because I can certainly redraw her shop up there."

"That's the map of Styx?" Emmaline asked, unable to believe her good luck.

"Of course. These silly goblins wouldn't know which way was north if I wasn't here to tell them, and they certainly wouldn't know where to rebuild their shops. Before I showed up, they were all fighting over the best locations in town."

"Delilah, we need to protect that map at all costs."

"Well, obviously," Delilah said. "Chaos knows we don't need a turf war on our hands."

"No, I mean we have to hide it, keep it safe. Sebastian…" she began, choosing her words carefully to keep her promise to Bostwick. "Sebastian is after it. He may be on his way here right now. He, well, he found a way to regain his old shape, and now I'm sure he has it in for Styx."

"Emmaline, he's not like that," Millicent said.

"You don't understand. He's not just some cat. He's an immortal beast, and—"

"Oh, Emmaline," Delilah said, petting her rabbit ears.

"Silly, silly, worrisome, silly Emmaline. I knows he's a mean little kitty, but why ever would he be after the map?"

"To destroy Styx! Why else?"

"What, am I invisible? Am I speaking Kobold?" Heather said, throwing her map to the ground. "For the last finger-licking time, only a true ruler of Styx can damage the map permanently!"

"But Sebastian *is* a true ruler of Styx."

They all stared at her, confused. Even Heather had nothing to say.

"I saw him, Delilah. He looks just like the goblin in that picture of the garden. The one standing next to the human."

"My," Delilah said, "he's lovely then, isn't he?"

"He's evil!"

"Give credit where credit is due. Why do you think it's him?"

"I saw him transform. He's paler and his eyes are different, but it's definitely him. And if he was in that painting, then that means he really is a member of the Styx royal family. He has the ability to wipe Styx off the map, literally. We can't let him get to it."

"You said he was on his way?" Heather asked, suddenly serious. "Then we should head straight back to the castle. Barricade it. Not let him anywhere near the map."

"Can you really keep him out of the castle? We don't know what kind of power he has."

"It'll be a start," Delilah said. "I'd much rather fight him where I have the advantage. Did you come by car?"

Millicent nodded and pointed. Delilah snatched a passing bugbear and asked if he could help them through the crowd.

He obliged by rolling into a ball and barreling through and over any goblin in his path. Within seconds, Delilah was leading Millicent, Emmaline, and Heather to the car. They only had to step over a fallen goblin once.

Bostwick considered himself to be already packed since all of his belongings fit magically into his hat. He decided, instead, to focus on Millicent's things. Not knowing when she would be done with her morning chores, he had to gather her belongings quickly so she couldn't warn Delilah.

It seemed like an excellent idea until he arrived at her room. Her shelves were crammed with books, dried flowers, and decorative knick-knacks. He opened her wardrobe to find dozens of dresses, mostly yellow, as well as the bright pink one. Would she want to bring clothes with her, he wondered, or maybe even an apron or two?

She'd apparently gone to Rare and Priceless a few more times, judging by several strange devices populating one corner of the room. Bostwick sorted through these, finding a silver teapot with mechanical spider legs sprouting from the bottom, two pairs of opera glasses, and a carved music box. These seemed to be the most Millicent-like items in the pile, and also happened to be the smallest, so he stuffed them into a nearby bag, which might very well have come from the counterfeit shop as well. He also shoved several dresses unceremoniously into the bag and turned to leave when something caught his eye.

On top of the wardrobe, far back against the wall, was a round, pink box. The color alone reminded him of Delilah, but he knew it couldn't have been her because Sebastian was now in possession of the Domino. Curious, he took the box down and opened the lid. Inside was a woman's top hat. It was smaller than usual, and would perch, pinned, on one side of the head, more like a decoration than a regular hat. This particular hat was made of a fabric the color of lemon cream, with a lacy green hatband.

Unlike the bizarre magical items from Rare and Priceless, Bostwick knew exactly what this was. Upon entering Melieh's Academy of Magic, every student was given a top hat to perform magic tricks with. They were traditionally black, though Bostwick knew a few students who had modified theirs. This hat was obviously the work of an expert milliner, the kind a girl might receive when she graduated. This, Bostwick knew, would be important to Millicent, so he took the hat, hatbox, and the bag of counterfeits to his room and nervously counted the minutes until noon.

"Shouldn't we barricade the door or something?" Heather asked once they had arrived safely in the throne room. Delilah went straight to the throne, followed by Millicent, who still carried Emmaline.

"No," Delilah said. "You should hold the map, but I want to face him head on, should he come here, which I doubt he's even gutsy enough to do. Especially if he has to face this!"

Delilah made a dramatic pose, and the domino on her face turned from plain black fabric to a mask of blue scales with a long snout.

"M-Millie," she said in a shaky voice, "do I look like a big wyrm?"

"No," the maid replied worriedly.

"I didn't think so. Well, how about this!"

The mask transformed again, into a bulbous pair of goggles with spiral streamers running down Delilah's face. She ripped the mask off, and it turned back to its black form.

"Phantasmal jellyfish are invisible, though," Delilah said, tuning the mask over and over. "Maybe it's broken. Did I use up its magic or something? Maybe Bostwick can fix it."

"Delilah, he…" Emmaline began, but couldn't finish.

"What is it, Emmaline?" Millicent said, turning the rabbit around in her arms to see her face to face. Emmaline looked away.

Millicent gasped and put Emmaline on the ground next to the throne, then silently walked to the side of the room.

"Where are you going?" Heather asked. "Shouldn't we all stay together?"

"I have to find Bostwick." She was about to open a secret door in the wall, but paused and looked back. "Delilah, you have to promise me something."

The queen seemed intrigued and tossed the mask onto the throne behind her.

"You have to promise that whatever happens, or happened, you won't curse Bostwick."

"I would never do such a thing, Millie! Ladies don't just curse people willy-nilly."

"Promise?"

Delilah nodded and Millicent turned to leave, but stopped when the throne room door was flung open.

♠♦♣♥♣♦♠

Bostwick went to the treasure chamber, where Sebastian was already waiting. He was wearing the blue and white military coat that had been hanging there. It fit him perfectly, and now that Bostwick thought about it, it might very well have belonged to him once.

"Are you ready?" Sebastian said, fastening the last of the buttons that ran down the front.

"Yes. But I don't know where Emmaline and Millicent are."

"They are most likely with Delilah in the throne room, I suspect. But don't worry, I'm ready for this. You'll be free before this day is out."

Sebastian walked over to where the sword with the black metal blade was displayed and took it in one hand. He looked over the blade appraisingly, then left the room. Bostwick ran to catch up to him as he sped toward the throne room with no signs of slowing down.

"Wait," Bostwick said breathlessly, "you aren't planning on killing her?"

"If all goes as planned, no one will be harmed. Believe me, I don't wish to kill anyone."

Bostwick was still unsure. It was true that Delilah wouldn't let them go without a fight, but he had never considered what that might entail on his part. Before he knew it, they were at the doors to the throne room, which Sebastian threw open, somehow, just by holding his hand out before him. Bostwick saw Delilah, Emmaline, and Heather gathered around the throne, holding a piece of paper, while Millicent stood off to the side, about to open one of the secret doors. They all froze as Sebastian entered, then Delilah jumped in front of Heather and Emmaline.

"So you decided to come here after all? " said the queen. "Well, you'll have to get through me first."

"What do you mean, Delilah? Surely, you don't think I came to kill a cartographer and a princess? I'm just here for the map," he said, looking coldly at the rabbit.

"You didn't go to the map shop at all, did you?" Emmaline said in disbelief. "You were just waiting for us to bring it here all along!"

"I knew you didn't trust me, Emmaline, and I figured that of all the places in Styx, this throne room is where you'd feel most secure."

His eyes narrowed, then he ran straight for Delilah. She conjured a glowing circle of light in front of her that emitted a humming, crackling sound. This somehow stopped Sebastian's sword, which would otherwise have gone straight through her.

"So we finally get to see some of your ancient Styx magic," he said, pushing the blade against her spell. "It won't help you this time, though."

Delilah looked him over, uttering a derisive "hmph".

Sebastian swung his sword up, trying to get around her shield, but she blocked again. Wherever he struck, Delilah placed her spell. She, Emmaline, and Heather were safe, but unable to move.

"How did you get back to your true form, anyway?" she asked.

Sebastian said nothing, but struck her shield over and

over again with his sword, though it showed no signs of weakening. He dropped his weapon to his side and smiled.

"I used your Domino. How else?"

Delilah at first looked confused, then enraged. She glanced over Sebastian's shoulder to Bostwick, who was too surprised to do anything, and for a few seconds, her spell faltered. Sebastian took this opportunity to swing his sword in towards her. She stepped back, barely avoiding it. She was unable to conjure the shield back fast enough, so Sebastian took the opportunity to step between her and Heather. Moving quick as lightning, Heather grabbed the map, rolled to her left and got back to Delilah.

"Give it here," the queen commanded. "I don't want anyone else getting involved in this fight."

Heather reluctantly obeyed, then ran to the edge of the throne room. Emmaline hid, as much as she could, behind the throne itself. Now, only Delilah stood in the center of the room, while Sebastian had one of his feet on the steps leading to the throne. They looked at each other, both silently fuming.

Bostwick saw something black shoot across the floor towards him and he had the sensation of something rushing past his face. The next moment, he realized that he was unharmed; only his hat had fallen, bottom up on the floor, seeming much further from him than it ought to be. Neither Sebastian nor Delilah had moved.

"You should realize," Sebastian said, "that this is the end of Styx. For too long, your family has arrogantly stood as the bridge between the human and the goblin worlds. Never again will you give goblin secrets to humans, never again will the world be polluted with your corrupt—"

"Oh, would you shut up," Delilah said.

"Styx *will* be destroyed!"

Sebastian ran for her again, keeping his sword low to the ground. Delilah was ready for him with a shield, but instead, he ran to his right, where Millicent stood, forgotten by everyone until now. Sebastian grabbed her around the waist with one arm, while with the other he held the sword to her throat.

"What are you doing?" Bostwick asked, but it came out as no more than a whisper.

"Tear up the map, or she dies," Sebastian said coldly.

Delilah stood still, her mouth slightly open, looking at Millicent, who trembled.

"Do it."

She looked at the map in her hands, then back at Sebastian.

"You're bluffing," she said, with her usual presumptuous tone.

Truly, it seemed as if killing Millicent was the last thing he wanted. His eyes had a wide, worried look, as if terrified he might have to make good on his ultimatum. Even so, he steadied his shaking hands and readjusted the sword, pressing its blade against the skin of Millicent's neck.

"Tear it apart," he said again. A tear rolled down Millicent's face.

"Delilah, you can't!" Emmaline cried, coming out from behind the throne. "You can't destroy Styx. It's your country!"

Delilah unfolded the map, studying it as if she could see

each and every goblin who lived in it. Then, staring defiantly at Sebastian, she tore it carefully into four pieces, then let what had once been the map of Styx flutter to the ground.

"Now let her go," Delilah commanded.

"Not part of the bargain," Sebastian said, and suddenly, waves of blackness—Sebastian's own shadow—shot from his feet to the pieces of the map on the floor. He collected them in his free hand at Millicent's waist as his shadow returned and took its place beneath him.

"Wait," Bostwick cried, finding his voice at last. "Let her go! You promised that we'd be free to go."

"You are free to go. Styx no longer exists."

And with that, Sebastian seemed to turn into wisps of black smoke and shadow, which enveloped the map pieces and Millicent in one swift motion, then streamed into Bostwick's hat on the floor, and were gone.

Delilah's shield spell flickered out. Both she and Bostwick were in a state of shock. The first one to speak was Emmaline.

"How could you?"

"I thought…" Bostwick began, but Emmaline cut him off.

"Not you, Bostwick, though you certainly have a lot to answer for. I mean you, Delilah. It doesn't matter if she was your friend. She was our friend, too, but you're the queen of a country. Do your citizens' lives mean nothing to you?"

Delilah had a far off, dazed expression, and seemed to hear nothing at all.

"And I suppose she should have just let Millicent die?" Bostwick said angrily.

"A queen's responsibility is to her people. I know Millicent was in trouble—"

"What do you mean 'was'?" Bostwick gasped, his voice breaking. "She's still in trouble. She's still... alive."

Though he sounded unsure. What had happened anyway? Where did things go when they entered a magician's hat?

Emmaline continued to berate Delilah about giving her country a veritable death sentence, but Heather, who was staring at her furry hands as if they ought not be there, cut her ranting short.

"I don't think she *did* destroy Styx. We're still here, aren't we?"

Emmaline was silent at once.

"I always imagined the destruction of the map to be more like an instant moment of devastation and then, BAM! Dead. But we seem to be perfectly okay. Maybe it didn't work. Delilah, did you—"

At that very moment, a great rumbling started. It sounded far off at first, but then the castle itself started to shake and shudder. It felt as if the walls around them would collapse at any instant, and then, suddenly, it stopped. They were brought to their knees with a crash. The sound of breaking glass brought all their eyes to the stained glass clock, which shattered, its yellow and green pieces streaming down into the gears like water, and behind them, the blue sky of Styx was not visible, but instead a murky brown smog could be seen behind winding, jagged towers and buildings.

Emmaline, Bostwick, and Heather ran to the window. Below them, they could see the garden and the dirt path that would have led to the town, but this stopped beyond the edge of the hedge maze and was replaced by filthy cobblestone streets, on which crowds of surprised goblins stood pointing up at the castle. All around them, buildings rose up like sentinels, black against the brown sky.

"Catawampus," Heather said. "I do believe we're in the capital of Catawampus."

"You mean we've been transported here?" Emmaline asked incredulously. "The entire castle? Well, what about the rest of Styx—is that all right?"

Heather thought for a moment.

"I've got it! Remember all that ranting Sebastian did before he left? About Styx being destroyed and not being the bridge between nations anymore? I'll bet my compass that he scattered the pieces of Styx all over Ataxia, leaving a great gap where it used to be. Of course! Because Delilah didn't destroy the map; she just tore it to pieces. The map still exists, as does what was drawn on it."

"What about Millicent?" Bostwick asked.

"I'm a mapmaker, not a mind reader. I've no idea why he took her away. Maybe it was just to hurt Delilah more. They were thick as thieves, those two."

Bostwick looked back at Delilah. It didn't make any sense. She had used and humiliated Millicent, stolen her memory away and lied to her, but then torn her country apart to save her. In the end, it was *his* fault that she had ever had to make that choice. He walked up to her slowly. She still seemed dazed by it all.

"Delilah," he began, but she punched him, extremely hard, in the arm. Her bony fist was like a mace.

"That's what you get for trusting a cat!" she said.

"Although you should get a lot worse for betraying me. And you, Emmaline. I should punt you out the window for your lack of faith."

"Delilah…"

"Didn't you know I knew what I was doing? Why do you think I tore the map where I did, hmm? Because of my careful planning, I kept the castle, the town, and the forest all intact in separate pieces. And the Wastes, of course. And yet you doubted me, acted like I didn't care about my own people. Really, I thought you knew me better than that."

"Sorry," Emmaline said sheepishly.

"Forgiven," Delilah said, "but I don't know about you, Bostwick. We'll have to discuss it further."

"But what about right now?" he asked. "What do we do about what's just happened?"

"Simple." She ran to the window, then spun around to face them. "All we have to do is retrieve the four pieces of the map, find some way to glue them back together and put them back in the right spot. Then, we hunt down Sebastian like the weasel he is, find Millicent, and make him pay for making her cry."

Here she breathed in the moist air that was coming in from the window as if breathing in everything she'd just said.

"This is going to be fun!"

The story continues in
The Styx Trilogy Book Two
Outcast Shadows
available for purchase in 2017

In the meantime,
find more information about
the Styx Trilogy (including bonus
stories about the characters)
at rosecorcoranwrites.com

Acknowledgements

Styx began as a doodle of Millie, Delilah, and Bostwick that I drew in the back of class, and nine years have passed since then. In that time, many people have helped to get this book into your hands, and I'd like to thank them.

Thank you, God, for not only giving me the talent to write and the obsession to stick with it, but for surrounding me with people who have helped me all along the way.

Thank you to my family, who have encouraged me this whole time. Thank you, Mom, not only for helping me with brainstorming and editing, but for raising me to be creative; you have no one to blame but yourself. Thank you, Dad, not only for being a big fan of my work, but also for being Bostwickian. Thank you, Claire, for letting me bounce ideas off you even though we have a hive mind and already share each other's thoughts, and also thank you for the awesome cover art and other illustrations. Thank you, Thomas, for helping me with technical and technological issues. And thank you to all my other family members who read my books in their early stages: John Paul, Laurel, Margo, and Aunt Ellie.

Thank you to my friends who have read some or all of my books in their various stages of development: Pauve,

Sarah, Cindy, Tony, Talamay, Missy, and Jennifer. Thank you, Michelle, not only for reading my book, but for helping me as a fellow writer; I look forward to reading your western. And, of course, thank you, Aaron, for reading my book "nine times".

The poem that Bostwick quotes from on page 164, Chapter 9, is "Only a Woman's Hair", written by Lewis Carroll. It a beautiful, thoughtful poem, and you should all go read it. Since he provided me not only with that poem, but endless inspiration, I thought it fitting to mention him here on the acknowledgements page. Thank you, Lewis Carroll!

About the Author

Rose Corcoran enjoys watching anime, taking hikes, and reading books. *Miscast Spells* is her first novel, but it won't be her last. She lives in Flagstaff, Arizona and drinks more tea than is normally considered acceptable.

To contact her, write to
rosecorcoranwrites@gmail.com

To contact the illustrator, Claire Corcoran, visit her Deviant Art page:
http://pennyfarthing1893.deviantart.com/